THE PIXY;

OR,

THE UNBAPTIZED CHILD.

A CHRISTMAS TALE.

BY

GEORGE W. M. REYNOLDS,

AUTHOR OF THE FIRST AND SECOND SERIES OF " THE MYSTERIES OF
LONDON," " FAUST," " THE DAYS OF HOGARTH," " WAGNER : THE
WEHR-WOLF," " THE CORAL ISLAND," " ROBERT MACAIRE,"
ETC. ETC. ETC. ETC.

BEAUTIFULLY ILLUSTRATED.

LONDON:

PUBLISHED, FOR THE PROPRIETOR, BY JOHN DICKS,
AT THE OFFICE OF " REYNOLDS'S MISCELLANY,"
WELLINGTON STREET NORTH, STRAND.

1848.

ADVERTISEMENT.

THIS tale is founded upon a popular superstition which until late years was very prevalent in Devonshire and Cornwall—to the effect, that the souls of young children who are unfortunate enough to die unbaptized, wander restlessly upon the earth, and haunt those scenes which were in any way associated with their short-lived existence.

CHAPTER I.

THE DEATH-BED.

In the neighbourhood of one of those small but picturesque towns which dot the champaign districts of the beautiful county of Devon, stood a retired but elegant little villa in the midst of a large garden. It would be impossible to conceive a more delightful residence than this, at that season of the year when the fragrant honey-suckle clustered over the portico, —when the woodbine dispensed its delicious perfume, —and when the adjacent hill, embowered at the eminence by a verdant grove, was melodious with the voices of the feathered choristers of the air. The wayfarer, as he passed along the road skirting the garden, would pause to refresh his eye with the roses that waved in blushing beauty—the tulips, that wore their most varied hues—the peonies that displayed their crimson pomp—and the lilies that seemed decked with the white robes of a bride. A crystal streamlet, crossed by a picturesque bridge, went babbling by the back of the elysian enclosure; and between this natural boundary and the hill stretched a rich pasture-land covered with flocks. The villa itself was of fanciful but pleasing cottage-architecture; and the interior was commodious and tastefully fitted up. Its proprietor and occupant was an attorney, whose offices were in the town; and as he was the only gentleman of that profession in the place, he had managed, during a long series of years, to realize a competency enabling him to retire from business in his old age. But certain family circumstances, with which we have nothing to do, rendered it necessary that he should remove to London; and he accordingly advertised his business and his beautiful villa for sale. The announcement was answered by a young gentleman of Exeter, named Lorimer; and a bargain having been concluded, the necessary documents were signed—the purchase-money was duly paid down—and the old lawyer, having thus surrendered his practice to the new one, took his departure for the metropolis, much regretted by those amongst whom he had dwelt for upwards of forty years.

As our readers may suppose, the inhabitants of the town of which we are speaking, but the name of which it is unnecessary to mention, were full of curiosity to learn anything and everything that related to the venerable attorney's successor. But at first the little which they could ascertain was to the effect that Mr. Lorimer was five-and-twenty years of age —that he had recently married a young, beautiful, and orphan girl at Exeter—and that he had embarked the small fortune which he inherited from his own deceased parents in the purchase of the business aforesaid, and the beautiful villa already briefly described. In due time Mr. and Mrs. Lorimer arrived from Exeter; and then the gossips of the town had an opportunity of passing their comments upon the personal appearance of the newly-married pair. All agreed that the lady, who could not have been more than seventeen, was one of the most lovely creatures on whom mortal eyes had ever settled. The luxuriance of her dark brown hair—the brilliancy of her complexion—the Grecian regularity of her features — the delicacy of contour which characterised her figure—and the grace which seemed to environ her entire person, instantly fascinated every beholder ; while her delicate and touching countenance, slightly expressive of melancholy, but bespeaking amiability of mind and goodness of disposition, won all hearts.

Concerning Mr. Lorimer, however, opinions were not quite so unanimous. His physiognomy, deriving its chief ornament from the large, dark, piercing eyes, appeared to be the transcript of a strong and vigorous intellect: but it likewise indicated a haughty and impetuous soul—and bore traces—even at that early age—of deep and violent passions. Some pronounced his features to be majestic and severe, and failed to observe in them any sinister expression: but all agreed that they were so strongly stamped as to denote a more than ordinary energy of the masculine character.

It was in the middle of summer when the newly-married pair arrived at the town and took possession of the villa. The principal families of the place lost no time in calling upon them; and the result of these visits led to the opinion that whereas Mrs. Lorimer was all sweetness, affability, and gentleness, her husband, even when striving to appear most courteous, could not shake off a certain reserve which was by some construed into haughtiness, and which was at all events habitual with him. In a short time it became apparent that the lawyer did not wish to mingle in society: but whether the secluded life which he preferred leading, arose from a naturally gloomy temperament—or from pride—or from an anxiety to devote all his leisure hours either to his wife or to study—was not immediately ascertained. That poverty or parsimony had no share in creating those retired habits, was however evident: inasmuch as the business which he had purchased yielded a competency, and the tradesmen with whom he dealt

were enabled to declare that no meanness characterised the domestic economy of the villa.

Six months passed away; and the blooming flowers
in the garden had perished upon the cold and turf-
less grave of winter.   But if the spot where the
Lorimers lived, now seemed to present a cheerless
contrast to its verdure and its gaiety in the warmer
seasons, comfort nevertheless reigned within the
walls of the dwelling.   Thick curtains afforded an
impervious barrier against the icy draughts; and the
atmosphere of the parlour was rendered genial by
means of the blazing logs heaped upon the hearth.
For sea-coal was not much used in the rural districts
at that time ;--and this observation reminds us of
the necessity of informing our readers that the period
of which we are writing was sixty years ago!

It was Christmas Day, 1788,—one of those Christmas Days which appear to have belonged only to the
" olden time,"—and not characterised by that damp,
rainy, and unwholesome weather which of late years
seems to have marked each anniversary of that
solemn festival with such inveterate regularity.   The

air was cold—but it was a crisp, dry, and bracing
cold that brought to the cheeks of youth the rosy
hues of vigorous health, and made the step of old age
firmer and more assured. Though the trees were
stripped of their leaves, yet the naked boughs seemed
not like the blackened skeletons of the garden and
the grove : for the transparent frost-work clung to
them like silver fringes, and in a thousand fantastic
shapes, as if woven by Nature's own curious hand.
The earth was as impenetrable as rock—the streamlet
had hardened into marble: and yet upon all the sun
shone forth—powerful enough to gladden the air,
but ineffectual to dissolve into pearly tears the icicles
that spangled the trees.

That Christmas Day was characterised by the usual
festivity at the town whereof we have been speaking;
—nor did the interior of the villa afford any excep-
tion in this respect. On the contrary, the Lorimers
had partaken of the good old seasonable fare; and
the young wife was rejoiced when her husband, un-
bending from his natural indifference relative to such
commonplace things, praised the various dainties

over the preparation of which she herself had presided. Evening came; and they drew their chairs
closer to the blazing hearth, and talked of the past
and speculated for the future in that familiar and delightful intimacy which husband and wife alone can
know. Never had Arthur Lorimer appeared more
affectionate—never more tender towards the charm-
ing Emily than on this occasion;—and when, in a
subdued and melting tone, she breathed fond hopes
relative to the babe of which in a few months' time
she expected to become the mother, he fixed upon
her a look more full of fervent affection than those
dark eyes had ever before expressed.

In this agreeable manner did the time pass away
until nearly ten o'clock, when the front-door bell
was suddenly rung with violence. A servant hastened to answer the summons; and she presently entered the parlour, to inform her master that a mes-
senger from the principal hotel in the town requested
to speak to him immediately. Lorimer ordered the
man to be admitted; and the object of the mission
was briefly explained. It appeared that a lady, who

only arrived at the hotel that afternoon, had been seized with such a sudden and alarming illness that the surgeon who had been called in to minister his aid, had recommended her to settle her earthly affairs, if she had any requiring such arrangement. She had expressed her desire to make a will; and it was for this purpose that Mr. Lorimer's presence was solicited without delay.

The lawyer bade the man return to the hotel with the assurance that he would speedily follow; and wrapping himself well up in his cloak, Lorimer embraced his wife and sallied forth. The cold was of a bitterness that seemed first to penetrate to the very marrow of the bones—then to numb the entire frame so as to render it incapable of feeling, and absorb the conviction of physical existence in the impression that the individual is but a *walking idea*. Hugging his mantle around him, Lorimer proceeded at a rapid rate; and in a quarter of an hour he reached the hotel. The landlord, on perceiving him, instantly commanded a chamber-maid to conduct him to the dying lady's room; and when they reached the threshold, Lorimer paused in the passage while the domestic entered to announce his arrival. In a few minutes she came forth, preceded by the surgeon, who shook his head with solemn intimation that all hope was gone. The chamber-maid and the doctor retired; and the lawyer passed into the room.

The door was so situated that the curtains of the bed concealed his form from the invalid, until, having laid aside his hat and cloak, he approached the couch with that gravity of demeanour which a professional man not only knows how to assume upon such an occasion, but which was natural to Arthur Lorimer. In the bed lay his perishing client—at that moment with her pale and death-marked countenance turned towards a child that was sleeping by her side, unconscious in its infant innocence of the doom that was sealed for its unhappy mother. She raised her head feebly : but scarcely had her eyes met those of Lorimer when a faint though agonising shriek escaped her lips — while, at the same instant, an ejaculation expressive of an equally unexpected and painful recognition, burst from him. He shivered and turned pale—then sank upon a chair by the bed-side; and the lady, covering her face with her hands, murmured, "My God! is this possible?—or is it a dream?" And then a long—a dead silence ensued in that chamber.

The dying woman was of remarkable beauty. In spite of the change which months of grief, and rage, and despair had worked in her, and which was now so fearfully enhanced by this sudden and overwhelming illness, Lorimer still recognised all the traces of that proud and imperious loveliness which he had once been wont to admire and which he had often complimented with so much apparent enthusiasm. For not even the icy touch with which the grim Destroyer heralded his approach, had been able to quench the fire of that eye which awed while it attracted, nor to dim the dark glory of that raven hair. Her age was about thirty: the style of her beauty was robust and masculine—full of loftiness—and indicating, in every feature, as stern a decision of character and passions as strong as might be read in the countenance of Lorimer himself.

We said that a long pause followed the sudden and most unanticipated recognition of the lawyer and that lady. On his part, vainly did the haughty soul seek to wrap itself up in its own dark pride and take refuge in a stern indifference: the chords of his heart vibrated to feelings which he could not subdue;—remorse for the past, terror for the present, and apprehension for the future created a tumult in his guilty breast. On the other hand, the dying woman pressed her brows with convulsive violence, to steady the thoughts that whirled in her brain: for she still doubted whether it were really *he*,—the man whom she had loved with so profound an affection, and had then hated with so bitter an aversion,—who was now present in that supreme hour when her spirit hovered between two worlds—the realm of Earth and the sphere of Heaven!

At length, as if resolved to clear up all doubt, she slowly turned towards him that countenance once so magnificently beautiful, but upon which the ghastly hues of mortality were now spreading fast; and, shuddering as she gazed, she said in a low and hollow tone, "It is not a dream—and at length we meet again, Arthur!"

"Are you pleased that we have thus met?" he asked, a cold tremor coming over him as his ear caught the sepulchral sound of that voice whose richness was so well remembered.

"Pleased!" she exclaimed with the bitterness of an energy temporarily reviving: "pleased!" she repeated, fixing a look of burning hatred upon the lawyer's countenance. "Yes—pleased to think that I may curse thee ere I die!" she added, a low but wildly ferocious laughter wavering upon her ashy lips.

"Just heaven! speak not thus, Margaret!" cried Lorimer, in a voice of consternation. "It is Christmas Day—the anniversary of a blessed event which should prompt the heart to forgiveness, and pardon, and mercy!"

"Oh! add not a vile hypocrisy to the full measure of your guilt, Arthur!" exclaimed the woman, upon whose lip not even the convulsions of dissolving nature could subdue the scornful sneer. "I am glad you reminded me that this was Christmas Day—for therewith have I so many, many bitter recollections associated. Was it not upon a Christmas Day—two years only have elapsed since *then* — that we first met? Tax your memory, Arthur—and call to mind how we encountered each other at the house of mutual friends—think of all the attentions you paid me,—bring back to recollection the interviews to which that first meeting led—the love that sprang up in *my* heart ——"

" And in mine," murmured the lawyer, agitated to the very depths of his soul, callous and selfish though it were.

" 'Tis false !—you never loved me !" ejaculated Margaret : " or else how could you have deceived me — how abandoned me at last, when you knew that I bore in my bosom a pledge of the illimitable love which my heart entertained for you? Oh! when I think of that love, I am lost in the contemplation of its infinity! It was a delirium—and it has gone! But by what sentiment has it been succeeded? By a hatred—an abhorrence — an aversion of equal

power, and far more deeply rooted! Yes, Arthur—
I hate you—and I have craved for vengeance, as the
expiring wretch on Afric's desert-waste longs for a
drop of water to cool his parched and blackening
tongue!"

"Oh! this is horrible—horrible!" exclaimed Lorimer, covering his face with his hands.

"Not so horrible as your perfidy is vile!" retorted
Margaret, a faint and hectic tinge appearing upon
her shrunken cheeks, as she raised herself painfully
up in the couch. "But the finger of Providence is
manifest in this, our last meeting upon earth!" she
added solemnly. "For it was on a Christmas Day,
two years ago, that we first beheld each other and
you whispered fond words in my ears. I loved
you—for I believed that you loved me; and a
twelvemonth passed like a dream of elysian bliss.
Another Christmas Day came—a year ago—and
then, for the first time likewise, you offered
up the incense of your perfidious heart to the
orphan, Emily Vavasour! Did I not overhear
your passionate declarations on that occasion?

—and did you not vow contrition and remorse ?
Another twelvemonth has gone — and, behold !
we meet again on a Christmas Day ! But during this last interval how much has happened to
make my heart a wreck and send me to an early
grave! In July last, while I was hourly expecting
to become a mother, in the retirement of that distant
village to which shame had driven me--you led my
rival to the altar. Then you quitted your native
city--you came hither, leaving no trace behind! Oh!
I comprehend it all now—yes—all, all! You buried
yourself and your young wife in the seclusion of this
town, in the hope to evade my vengeance;—for you
knew me well enough, Arthur," she added, the hot
breath coming in clouds from her dilating nostrils,--
" to be aware that my ardent love would turn to as
fierce a hate! Yes—you sought to elude me : but
heaven itself has interposed to bring us together
again—if only for a few minutes—ere I die!"

With these words, Margaret sank back exhausted
—again covering her face with her hands.

Lorimer was shocked—appalled: he was rivetted

to his seat—his tongue refused to give utterance to
the prayer for pardon which his feelings urged him
to proffer—his flesh crept, chill and snake-like, upon
his bones. His eyes fell upon the countenance of the
sleeping child—a girl of only five months : but no
father's emotions sprang into existence in his bosom.
He even loathed the babe, as if it were the cause of
this terrific scene through the ordeal of which he
was destined to pass.

"See to what your treachery has reduced me!"
suddenly exclaimed Margaret, life rallying yet again:
and she removed her hands from her countenance.
"Where is the beauty that thou wast once wont to
praise with such enthusiasm? Withered—gone!
Where is the strength of mind that enabled me to
dare all'and everything for thy sake? Thou hast
trampled it as a reed beneath thy feet! Where is
that heart which once throbbed so powerfully for
thee? Thou hast broken it into shivers as if it were
glass! But heed well what I am about to say to
thee, Arthur Lorimer! The Christmas season, which
to others is a blessing, shall become to thee a curse:

for thou hast forfeited all claim to that salvation and
that mercy which He who was born on that day,
came into the world to ensure on behalf of his elect!
Oh! I feel—I feel that I am suddenly gifted with the
powers of a Pythoness," she exclaimed, her eyes
lighting up with the fever of delirium; "and I tell
thee, Arthur Lorimer, that whatever evil this world
has in store for thee, shall assuredly overtake thee on
the day which thou hast desecrated with thy perfidy!
Dread, then, the anniversary of a day so full of hope
to other men—so replete with dark menace for thee!"

"Spare me, Margaret—spare me!" exclaimed the
unhappy man, writhing beneath denunciations to
which the very presence of death gave such awful
solemnity and such harrowing effect. "Spare me, I
say—if not for my sake—at least for that of the child
who slumbers by your side——"

"And this child is your own!" said the lady, her
voice suddenly becoming melting and tender, as she
bent a look of impassioned fondness upon the babe.
"But will you perform a father's part towards her?"
she asked, suddenly.

"I will," he answered, in a solemn tone.

"Know, then, that our child is as yet unchristened—as yet unnamed," she proceeded, in a low but impressive whisper: "and this neglect—which was not however all neglect, but partly shame — weighs heavily on my soul. For art thou ignorant of the belief which pervades our native Devonshire, and in regard to which I dare not prove a sceptic? Saith not the legend that the souls of those infants who die unbaptized, wander restlessly upon the earth—haunt the scenes with which their brief existence was in any way associated—and work weal or woe for them whom they might have had reason to love or hate? Yes—this is the belief: and it were terrible —terrible if this innocent babe were doomed to eternal exclusion from the realms of bliss!"

"The child shall be baptized—by your own name, Margaret," said Lorimer, awed by a superstition which at any other time and in different circumstances he would have discarded with contempt. "But have you no instructions—no last wishes to enjoin—no affairs to settle——"

"Ah! you would exercise your professional avocations even here—by my death-bed?" exclaimed the lady, the plaintive expression which her countenance had recently assumed, changing to that scornful air which was terrible to contemplate in one perishing so rapidly. "You know that I am rich, Arthur—and you—you——"

"By heaven! you wrong me," he cried. "I thought not of myself! How could I dare expect or hope that, while still writhing beneath the bitter denunciations which you have poured forth against me——But, my God! she is dying!" he almost shrieked out, as he started from his chair and seized her hand, which he pressed to his lips, with a fervour that was not altogether assumed.

"No—no——never—never again——caresses from *you!*" she murmured faintly, but withdrawing her hand forcibly, as her glazing eyes were for an instant animated with the ominous fire of a malignant hate. "Fulfil your destiny——it will be terrible——but you are forewarned——and dread a Christmas Day ——Arthur——my child——*our* child——Mary——

my dearest sister——pardon——O heaven! have mercy upon me!"

With these words she gave a last gasp—and in another instant the broken-hearted Margaret became one of the great congress of the dead!

CHAPTER II.

THE SISTERS.

How different was the scene passing on that very same evening in a humble cottage fifty miles distant, and in the immediate neighbourhood of the ancient city of Exeter. It was indeed, as we have declared, a humble dwelling: but the storm of guilty passions raged not within its walls. Peace, mental tranquillity, contentment, and love were depicted upon the countenances of the young peasant-couple that sate by the cheerful hearth; and as they bent upon each other looks of the most devoted attachment, they discussed their little projects for the future in the full assurance that a beneficent Providence would bless their endeavours to gain the bread of honest industry, even as they blessed His name for the past proofs of divine goodness which they had experienced.

James Doyle was a farm-labourer who, thanks to the thrift of worthy parents, had inherited a little cottage with an acre of ground attached, and who thus possessed some small means in addition to the wages which he earned from 'Squire Jackson, who owned the vast estate on the border of which his own miniature patch of land was situated. James was about six-and-twenty years of age; and a few months previously to the present date, he became the happy husband of a young woman to whom he had long been engaged. Mary Pennant had been an under-nursery-maid in the service of Mr. and Mrs. Jackson, who were kind and good people; and as there was something tinged with romance in the history of the girl, she had been the object of a more than ordinary interest in the estimation of her master and mistress.

In terms as concise as possible we will make our readers acquainted with the particulars thus alluded

to. Margaret and Mary Pennant were the daughters
of a humble tradesman dwelling at Exeter. There
was a difference of about six years between the ages
of the girls, Margaret being the elder: and there was
a still wider distinction betwixt their dispositions and
their personal appearance. For, whereas Margaret
was a dark beauty, Mary was one of those lovely
pensive, light-haired, blue-eyed maidens on whom it
was impossible to gaze without a feeling of tender
yet pure and holy interest; and whereas the elder
sister was of strong passions and an imperious soul,
the younger was surrounded by a halo of innocence
in which the looks of the libertine were subdued
into respectful admiration ere they fell upon her
angelic countenance. While the girls were still of
tender age — Margaret being thirteen and Mary
seven—their mother died; and shortly afterwards
their father, Mr. Pennant, being an improvident man
and overwhelmed with pecuniary difficulties, fled
from Exeter, leaving his daughters to the care of
his maiden-sister—a good, kind-hearted woman, who,
though possessed of but very limited means, cheer-

fully undertook the guardianship of her nieces. Six or seven years passed away, during which an occasional letter was received from Mr. Pennant, who had settled in India; and each missive contained the intelligence that his prospects were gradually improving, but that he was as yet unable to send remittances to aid in the education of his daughters. At length, when Margaret was twenty-one and Mary fifteen, a letter arrived containing money, and requesting that Mr. Pennant's elder daughter might be sent out to him at Calcutta; the epistle observing that " he would cheerfully have both his dear children with him as speedily as possible, but that he could not think of depriving his kind sister of the society of the younger and more tender plant." He likewise gave instructions to ensure the comfort and protection of Margaret during the voyage to India; and the elder daughter accordingly took leave of her affectionate aunt and disconsolate sister, and repaired to London, whence she shortly embarked on board of one of the Company's ships, the captain's wife (who accompanied her husband) taking charge of her according to a previous arrangement.

Not many months had succeeded the departure of Margaret Pennant for that far-off Asiatic clime where British oppression and aggrandizement have gone hand in hand, when a malignant epidemic visited the city of Exeter; and the worthy aunt became one of its earliest victims. Thus, at the tender age of scarcely sixteen, the innocent and artless Mary was left friendless and unprotected in her native city. So soon as her grief for the loss of her beloved relative was somewhat tranquillised — or rather mellowed into the melancholy of a pious resignation—she seriously thought of following her sister to India: but when her deceased aunt's little personal property was sold (her income having died with her) there was only a bare sufficiency to pay the funeral expenses and the liability contracted with the medical attendant during her illness. Mary was therefore compelled to abandon the project of repairing to India, until she could communicate with her father. But in the meantime she must do some-

thing to earn her bread; and she resolved to go out
to service. By the recommendation of one of the
tradesmen with whom her aunt had been accustomed
to deal, she applied to Mr. and Mrs. Jackson, who
were in want of an under-nursery-maid at the time;
and the vacant situation was immediately conferred
upon her.

Months—and even years passed; and Mary received no tidings either of her father or her sister.
One letter—and only one—had reached her since
Margaret's departure; and that was written the
moment the latter had landed at Calcutta, to announce her safe arrival. But to the epistle which
Mary had penned to convey the intelligence of her
aunt's death and solicit her father's advice and instructions, no answer was returned. Again and
again did she write: still no response came;—and at
length she discontinued her unavailing letters. But
the reader may well conceive that this silence on
the part of her father and sister was a source
of deep affliction to the young maiden, whose affectionate disposition yearned to be relieved from a

cruel suspense concerning those who were so dear to her; and often and often was her sleepless pillow moistened with tears. However, in the kindness of Mrs. Jackson she experienced no small degree of consolation; and then came her acquaintance with James Doyle, whose frank and manly nature, excellent qualities, and handsome person in due time won the heart of the gentle Mary.

It was about three years previously to the opening of our tale, and when Mary was twenty-one, that she was informed a lady requested to speak to her in Mrs. Jackson's drawing-room. To that apartment she repaired; and on crossing the threshold, she found herself in the presence of an elegantly-dressed female, who, rushing towards her, clasped the astonished maiden in her arms. Thus was it that the sisters again met—after a separation of six long years! But we must not dwell too long upon this affecting scene: vain were it to attempt to describe the effusion of tenderest feelings that now took place—vain would be any endeavour on our part to depict the thoughts that swarmed forth from their souls like bees from a hive. Mary's history was soon told: that of Margaret was not equally brief—nor was it as truly and faithfully related. There was however one fact in the narrative of the latter which plunged her gentle sister into the most poignant grief: and this was the announcement that their father was no more!

But let us pause for a few moments to glance at the career of Margaret Pennant in India. When her sire had written for her to repair to Calcutta to join him, his circumstances were so desperate, through his wonted improvidence, that he was barely able to make the remittance necessary for the payment of her passage. But having learnt, through his sister's letters, that Margaret had grown up into a young woman of surpassing loveliness, he sent for her with a view to one of those matrimonial speculations to which English parents settling in India so frequently have recourse. Accordingly, within a very few weeks after Margaret's arrival, she was married to a wealthy merchant, old enough to be her grandfather; and Mr. Pennant obtained the wherewith to amend his broken fortunes. Immediately after her union with Mr. Gordon, Margaret was compelled to accompany him to Madras, where his principal place of business was established; and there she became the star of fashion in the English society of the Presidency. Courted and flattered, complimented and worshipped by the gay young officers of the garrison, her head was turned with this change in her position: the incense of adulation made her giddy; and her naturally ardent temperament soon carried her astray. She eloped with a dashing captain in a regiment that was ordered to a very distant settlement in the interior; and for upwards of four years she lived with her paramour. Shame prevented her from writing to her father: much less did she venture to pen a line to her sister in England. At length she received the news that her husband had died suddenly and intestate; and, abandoning the captain of whom she was by this time wearied, she proceeded to Madras. There she took possession of the deceased Mr. Gordon's property; and, having realised it, hastened to Calcutta.

But on arriving at the capital of the Anglo-Indian
territory, she learnt that her father had been carried
off long previously, and after a few hours' illness,
by that appalling scourge—the CHOLERA! By com-
paring dates, she found that his demise must have
taken place within three weeks after her marriage,
and while she was journeying with her husband from
Calcutta to Madras.   On inquiring in the proper
quarter, she discovered that several letters had arrived from England addressed, some to her father
and some to herself; and these were from her long-
neglected, but never-forgotten sister Mary.   They
contained the intelligence of the aunt's death, and
likewise stated that the friendless maiden had been
compelled to enter a state of servitude to earn her
bread.   Oh! what bitter tears did Margaret Gordon
shed over those touching epistles, to which she knew
that no answer had ever been sent!   But she wasted
no time in useless grief: she longed to return to her
native land—to revisit the city of her birth—to
embrace her sister Mary!   Her preparations for
departure were soon made; and she embarked on

board the very same ship that had brought her out upwards of five years back, but which had performed several voyages to and fro since then.

The passage was long and tempestuous: but at length Margaret, laden with wealth, set foot upon the British soil. She sped to Exeter; and her first care was to visit her sister.

Such was the real outline of the lady's career in India: but she confessed not all its details to Mary. Her shame and her guilt she studiously concealed— alleging some reason, which obtained ready belief on the part of the unsuspecting Mary, for her long silence in respect to epistolary correspondence. The particulars of the above narrative will moreover have explained to the reader how it was that the poor girl's letters had remained unanswered.

And now, when a thousand questions had been put and responded to on either side, Margaret said, "Come, dearest sister: my carriage is waiting at the door to bear you hence. Take leave of those who, as you declare, have been kind to you; and hasten away from a scene of servitude in which you have lingered too long. I am rich—and henceforth we will dwell together in luxury and happiness."

But Mary, throwing herself into her sister's arms, and hiding her blushing countenance upon that bosom over which the costliest jewellery festooned, murmured a confession of the love which she bore for a humble peasant, and of the mutual vows which they had exchanged. Margaret's proud disposition revolted at the thought of her sister becoming the wife of a man in so lowly a position; and she even chid her harshly for entertaining the bare idea. Then the young maiden exhibited a firmness of character which had never revealed itself before; and with an earnest eloquence, she declared that not only did she respect the pledges which she had given, but that her happiness was dependent on the realisation of the hopes which her heart had cherished. Vainly did Margaret persuade—reproach—implore —and threaten by turns: Mary remained resolute— although her determination was proclaimed amidst torrents of tears that fell in deep regret at this variance of opinion between two sisters who

had only just been united after so long a separation. Margaret, piqued to the very soul at
what she termed her sister's " obstinacy," requested
that the subject might not be farther alluded to on
the present occasion; and she bade her sister hasten
to accompany her, inwardly hoping that the gaiety
and pleasure of "good society" would speedily induce the maiden to abandon all thoughts of bestow-
ing her hand upon the peasant. But the young
woman's sentiment was of that pure and holy nature
which rendered it indestructible: though every other
feeling of the heart might be obliterated, this one
at least could never die;—and with it was associated a discernment enabling her to recognise the
impropriety of her suddenly throwing off the stuff
gown of a menial and assuming the silken dress of
a lady, so long as she seriously and firmly contem-
plated the fulfilment of her sacred pledge to James
Doyle, the peasant.

"No, dearest Margaret," she said, the tears still
streaming from her eyes: "I am no longer a fit
companion for you! Our ideas are so different—

such a wide gulf exists between the spheres in which
we respectively move, that I should experience no
real happiness in entering upon a life of indolence
and ease;—while, on the other hand, were I to embrace your kind proposal, you would often have to
blush for the awkwardness, embarrassment, and
diffidence of your sister.   My destiny is fixed: I
shall become the wife of the man who loves me, and
whose generous nature I can so well appreciate;—
and until the day arrives for me to accompany him
to the altar, I will remain in my present position.
My best—my sincerest—my most fervent wishes
attend upon thee, dear sister: but I may not go
with thee hence."

And it was thus that Margaret and Mary sepa-
rated—the former scarcely able to restrain an out-
burst of her impetuous passion, and the latter con-
soled with the consciousness of having performed
her duty.   With that candour which was a part of
her amiable nature, did she reveal to her mistress—
and subsequently to James Doyle—all that had
passed between herself and her sister;—and al-

though Mrs. Jackson, as a woman of the world,
would not have persuaded the young maiden to
adopt a course which was in itself a rejection of
numerous advantages suddenly presented to her
view, yet she could not but admire and praise the
strict integrity of principle and truthfulness of mind
which had influenced her conduct. As for the
humble peasant—those who have loved well and
devotedly, can best appreciate all that he felt and
imagine all that he said, when he learnt, with indescribable rapture and touching gratitude, the
immense sacrifice which his worshipped Mary had
that day made for him.

From that time forth the sisters saw each other
but seldom. Once or twice did Margaret call to
renew her persuasions and her remonstrances: but
finding that Mary was inexorable in that respect,
she suddenly experienced a feeling of indifference—
not unmingled with contempt — for the young
woman whose notions, tastes, and inclinations she
looked upon as vulgar, grovelling, and low. Then
came the gay lady's connexion with Lorimer; and

absorbed in her new passion, she almost ceased to remember that there was such a person in the world as Mary Pennant.

It was while Margaret Gordon had retired into a strict seclusion to conceal from the world the results of her amour with the lawyer, that Mary accompanied James Doyle to the altar. It was a humble but a happy wedding; and if there were a single cause for regret on the part of the bride, it was the absence of her sister whom she had not now seen for a long, long time. The kind-hearted Mrs. Jackson provided the marriage-feast, which was done ample justice to by many sincere friends of the newly-wedded pair; and when the peasant bore his blushing wife home to the cottage in the evening, they were followed by wishes more fervent and sincere than those which are often breathed by hollow-hearted aristocrats and ladies of fashion at St. George's, Hanover Square.

By a singular coincidence, this union took place in the same month that Arthur Lorimer led Emily Vavasour to the altar;—and thus the younger sister was rendered supremely happy by him to whom her heart's pure and holy affections were given, at the very time when the object of Margaret's guilty amour was contracting a marriage which blighted all the wretched woman's hopes for ever. And now, too, while that elder sister—so proud and haughty, and yet so frail—was perishing miserably on the evening of a Christmas Day,—Mary—so meek, so amiable, and so good—was seated happily by her husband's side, at the hearth of that cottage where contentment, peace, and sweet affection had made their beatific home.

CHAPTER III.

LORIMER AND THE DOYLES.

IT was a week after the memorable Christmas Day upon which our tale opens, that a post-chaise drove up one forenoon to the door of the humble cottage in the neighbourhood of Exeter; and a gentleman, alighting from the vehicle, entered the house and inquired if that were the residence of Mrs. Doyle. It was to Mary herself that this question was put; and she immediately satisfied the stranger that he was speaking to the very person for whom he had asked. He then proceeded to inform her that his name was Lorimer—that he was an attorney practising at a certain town about fifty miles distant—and that it was his unpleasant duty to impart to her the death

of her sister at an hotel in the place which he had
mentioned.

Mary was dreadfully affected upon receiving this
intelligence; and it was some time before she could
so far compose herself as to solicit any details respecting the melancholy event. But when she was
sufficiently tranquiiiised to resume her conversation
with Lorimer, he informed her that Mrs. Gordon,
while travelling in a post-chaise in a private manner,
had been seized with so sudden and alarming an illness at the town alluded to, that she was compelled
to alight at the hotel, where death speedily over-
took her.

" When she found that her last hour was approach-
ing," continued Mr. Lorimer, " she requested that a
lawyer might be sent for, as she was anxious to give
him some instructions. I was accordingly summoned
to the death-bed of the lady; and she bade me take
charge of her papers, which were in her writing-
desk, and which would afford a clue to the little property which she had remaining. For she informed
me that, though she had passed as a woman of

wealth, she had never in reality possessed any large means, and that her limited resources had been almost completely exhausted by her extravagant mode of life. It was pride which had induced her to affect that ease of circumstances; and it was an habitual luxuriousness which made her persist in a lavish expenditure until the last."

"My poor sister!" murmured Mary, her utterance almost choked with sobs.

"She spoke kindly—very kindly of you," continued Lorimer, "and begged that I would visit you to impart the sad tidings of her death, so that you might be spared a sudden shock by receiving the intelligence through any indirect channel. She implored that you would forgive her for any harshness or unkindness on her part——"

"Oh! never—never, for a single instant, did I entertain an angry feeling towards her!" sobbed poor Mary, the tears running down her cheeks.

"You have at least that consolation, Mrs. Doyle, in your present affliction," observed the lawyer, assuming a tone of deep commiseration. "Your

sister loved you dearly—and in her last moments
she wished, for your sake, that she was indeed
as wealthy as the world believed her to be. But
what little she has left, and which consists chiefly—
as I am informed—of furniture, plate, and books at
her house in Exeter, and of the jewellery and clothes
which I have brought with me in the post-chaise,—
those effects are bequeathed to you. The papers
which I found in her writing-desk, speak of a
hundred pounds or so, vested in some security in
London; and as I am about to visit that metropolis
in a few days, on business of mine own—I will attend
to that little matter for you at the same time. On
my return into Devonshire, which will be in about
three weeks, I will make it a point to call upon you
again and place in your hands the amount that may
be forthcoming."

Mr. Lorimer spoke in so straight-forward, com-
passionate, and kind a manner, that Mary knew not
how to say enough in order to testify her gratitude
for the sympathy which he showed and the trouble
he was taking in her behalf. At this stage of the

interview her husband returned from the fields to his dinner; and Mary began to communicate to him the intelligence which the attorney had brought her: but her grief revived with suffocating effect—and Mr. Lorimer was himself obliged to take up the tale. He repeated all that he had previously stated to Mary, and reiterated the account which he had given of the deceased lady's property. He moreover observed that the funeral had taken place with the utmost privacy, according to a desire which she expressed with her latest breath; and that it was also in obedience to her dying wish that the melancholy tidings of her departure from this world were not communicated to her sister until after the ceremony of the obsequies.

Doyle, who was as unsuspecting and frank-hearted as his wife, not only put implicit faith in everything which Lorimer said, but likewise expressed his thanks for the interest he took in the matter: so that when the lawyer produced two or three papers, which he requested both Mary and her husband to sign, alleging that they were mere formal documents empowering him to act in their behalf, the worthy couple affixed their signatures without the slightest hesitation. Mr. Lorimer's clerk, who accompanied him in the post-chaise, was summoned to witness them; and the attorney promised that he would realise for them the personal property in the house at Exeter without delay, and that he would hand them over the proceeds thereof before he went to London.

A large trunk was now fetched from the vehicle and deposited in the cottage; and Lorimer, having intimated that it contained the clothes and jewels to which he had already alluded, took his leave.

It will be seen that he did not mention a single word relative to the child which Margaret had left behind her : for he was well assured that Mary was ignorant of her sister's shame — and he did not choose to enlighten her upon that head. For, had he done so, she would naturally have instituted inquiries to ascertain who was the father of the babe; and, although his amour with Margaret had been conducted with so much secrecy that if was scarcely even suspected in Exeter, nevertheless such inquiries might elicit facts which would gradually lead to the discovery of the whole truth. In this case, the Doyles would look upon him with suspicion and distrust: whereas it now suited his purposes to acquire and retain their implicit confidence, so as to keep entirely in his own hands the management of their business relative to the deceased lady's property.

That the name of Lorimer was unknown alike to Doyle and his wife until this occasion, and that they had never even heard of such a person having been on terms of intimacy with Mrs. Gordon at Exeter, need not appear surprising, when it is recollected that the man himself was so engaged from morning to night in his honest toils that he seldom set foot within the precincts of the city, and that little or no ntercourse had existed between the sisters since the first two or three visits which the elder one had paid the younger at Mr. Jackson's house. On the other hand, that Lorimer should not only have known that Margaret had so near a relative living as Mary, but

should likewise have been acquainted with every
particular respecting the position of the latter, may
naturally be inferred from his close intimacy with
the unfortunate woman who had loved him so fondly.

On leaving the Doyles, Lorimer and his clerk
proceeded in the post-chaise to Exeter, where they
stopped at the house of the late Mrs. Gordon. An
old female domestic was alone in charge of the
premises: for Margaret had not lived there since
the period of her retirement into a strict seclusion
to conceal her shame; and previous to leaving it for
that purpose, in the early part of the year, she had
dismissed all her dependants save the old house-
keeper, alleging that she was about to travel for
some months. To this woman Lorimer's business
was soon explained: her mistress was dead—and he
represented the heirs-at-law. Her wages were paid
with liberality; and she took her departure, weeping
for the loss of Mrs. Gordon. A valuation was then
made of the effects; and the lawyer was careful in
having this process conducted in the most straight-
forward manner. A sale followed; and the assets

realised amounted to a couple of hundred pounds, vouchers being duly drawn up to confirm the results. This business occupied three days; and Lorimer then returned to the cottage, where he paid over the money to the Doyles, retaining only a very small fee for himself so as not to appear *too disinterested* in the matter. He even insisted upon going over the account with Mary's husband, and bade him examine every voucher; and thus he fully confirmed these worthy and unsuspecting people in the good opinion which they had already formed of him. Their signatures were required to one or two more papers, connected with the sum of money to be recovered in London; and Lorimer again took his leave, with a promise to revisit them so soon as he came back from the great metropolis.

Three days afterwards the lawyer arrived in London; and for nearly a week he was occupied with the business which had taken him thither. His visits to stockbrokers, and with them to the Bank of England, were frequent during that interval: for there were large sums of money to receive

and dispose of—transfers to make—and an infinite
variety of financial arrangements to complete. His
presence was likewise needed on several occasions
at the India House, and also with the English agent
for a great commercial firm at Calcutta: in fine,
he appeared to have been entrusted with weighty
and important affairs—and he lost no time in bring
ing them to a settlement.

On his return into Devonshire he stopped at the
Doyles' cottage in his way homeward; and, in a
business-like manner, he informed them that the
sum to which they were entitled was nearly double
the amount he had at first anticipated: but he
assured them that he had experienced considerable
difficulty in obtaining it at all, so many legal
technicalities were there to overcome and so much
unforeseen difficulty to encounter. The gratitude
of James and Mary Doyle rose in proportion to the
trouble which their affairs had evidently occasioned;
and the worthy peasant strove to press upon the
lawyer a gratuity of twenty guineas above the few
pounds which he charged for his expenses. But

Lorimer persisted in declining the present, declaring that he was sufficiently well paid already by the other matters which had taken him to London, and that while engaged in attending thereto he had experienced a comparatively trifling inconvenience in devoting an occasional half-hour to their little business. Finally, he took his leave of the Doyles, pausing however for a moment upon the threshold of the cottage-door to advise them, with a friendly air, to be careful how they used their money and rather to lay it out by degrees than provoke the envy and jealousy of their neighbours by disbursing it all at once. They deemed the counsel to be as good as they imagined it to be honestly proffered and well-meant; and Lorimer took his departure, attended by the fervent gratitude of the ingenuous couple.

The lawyer returned home, where he experienced the most affectionate welcome from the amiable Emily, in whose arms reposed the dead Margaret's child—that child which was also *his own!* But Mrs. Lorimer suspected not that she was fondling the offspring of her husband's guilty amour: indeed, of that amour itself she was utterly ignorant. She had been slightly acquainted with Mrs. Gordon at Exeter; but never in her artless soul had arisen the suspicion that there was any improper connexion between that lady and Arthur Lorimer;—nor had she now been informed that it was none other than this same Mrs. Gordon who had so recently died at the hotel, and whose child was bequeathed to her care. For Margaret was travelling at the time under a feigned name; and thus every circumstance lent its aid to the attorney to conceal all he chose to suppress in reference to his amour with the deceased.

The explanation which he had given to his wife was that the lady to whose death-bed he had been summoned was a Mrs. Jocelyn—the widow of a wealthy East India merchant; and that being utterly friendless in this country, she had implored him— when finding herself past all hope, and having pre- viously ascertained that he was a married man—to take charge of her infant child. It was not, he added, a mere appeal to his benevolence that was thus made—but likewise to his own peculiar interests: inasmuch as the lady left at his disposal ample resources not only to remunerate him well for the rearing and education of *the orphan*, but also to endow her with a handsome settlement on her arrival at her majority. Lorimer moreover observed that the infant's name was Isabella; and all these statements did he make with such an air of candour and truthfulness, that not for a single instant did the artless Emily behold anything extraordinary or suspicious in them. She had therefore adopted the child with a heartfelt pleasure; and when her husband returned from London, he found her fondling it as if it were her own.

It will be recollected that he had sacredly pledged himself to the dying Margaret to have the babe christened; but now that she was no more, and that the superstitious influence of the words which she used on that occasion had passed away from the mind of the attorney, he hesitated not to break his solemn vow. For how could he have the babe baptized, without exciting the strangest suspicions on the part of his wife, and affording food for the gossip of the towns-folk? He had already declared that *the orphan's* name was Isabella: and he had led Emily to believe that it was legitimately born. Was it probable, then, that a child upwards of five months old should not have already undergone the holy ceremony, when (according to his representations) there were no motives to induce its mother to observe any mystery respecting its birth? But to have it baptized *now*, would be to give room for conjecture and speculation relative to the cause why the rite had never been performed before; and, for numerous reasons, Lorimer was desirous that no extraordinary degree of curiosity should be awakened with regard to the babe or its deceased mother.

Time wore on — months passed away; and at length Emily Lorimer presented her husband with a fine boy. Upon the right arm of the new-born child, midway between the elbow and the shoulder, appeared a small but very peculiar mark resembling a mulberry stain; and this little circumstance, trivial as it may now seem, the reader will have the kindness to keep in view, as it may hereafter become an important fact. The babe was baptized by its father's name of Arthur; and no mother was ever more proud of her first-born, nor more devotedly attached to it, than the tender and affectionate Emily.

Almost at the same time—at the cottage near Exeter, fifty miles distant—James and Mary Doyle became the happy parents of a daughter; and they bestowed upon the infant the name of Margaret, in remembrance of one whose image the surviving sister so fondly cherished, and whose frailty was unknown alike to her and her husband.

CHAPTER IV.

THE INCIDENTS OF TWO CHRISTMAS DAYS.

A YEAR had passed away from the date mentioned at the opening of our tale; and the sun dawned upon Christmas Day, 1789. But sorrow filled the heart of Emily Lorimer: for her little charge, Isabella Jocelyn, lay at the point of death, after an illness which had already lasted three weeks. The attorney's wife, naturally possessing so good a heart, had learnt to love the child as if it were her own offspring; and all the care and attention which an affectionate woman could bestow in such a case, had been lavished by her upon the infant sufferer. How different was it with her husband! *His* callous soul remained untouched—unmoved by the knowledge that Death was already standing by the cradle of the little girl : and although it was *his own daughter* who had been thus wasting and was now perishing before his eyes, yet beneath the aspect of sorrow which for decency's sake he assumed, there was a positive rejoicing in his heart at the thought that the merciless Destroyer was about to bear away the innocent one whom he had always looked upon as an intruder.

Oh! catch, as by a daguerreotype, a view of the heart of MAN, and a representation of that of WOMAN,—contrast them—place them in juxta-posi-tion—compare the feelings and the passions which harbour in the first, with the holy sympathies that quiver with such everlasting intensity in the latter, and then confess that the lord of the creation is but a savage barbarian by the side of that being of the gentler sex whom he stigmatises as frail, fickle, in-constant, and capricious! As the dark cloud in the stormy north is to the pure moonlight on the bosom of the Mediterranean,—as the crashing of heaven's artillery is to the harmony of the spheres,—and as the lurid glare of the volcano is to the eternal radiance that prevails in Paradise—so is the heart of arrogant and presumptuous MAN to that of oppressed and maligned WOMAN!

Throughout that Christmas Day did Emily Lorimer remain watching by the side of the tender infant whose life was ebbing away fast as the sand in an hour-glass. The doctor declared that all his skill was baffled, and that all the resources of his art were now unavailing: for nothing short of a miracle could rescue Isabella Jocelyn from death. Wearily —sadly—heavily passed the day: many and bitter were the tears which Emily wept over the sweet face on which a sickly smile played ever and anon, as the glazing blue eyes — those eyes recently so bright and beautiful — met her own. As evening came the child grew worse; and now, seated close by the fire, Emily held it in her arms—pressing it to her bosom—weeping over it—and uttering, amidst almost suffocating sobs, the tenderest and fondest things. Even for the time her own little Arthur was neglected! But the miracle that could alone redeem the suffering Isabella from the jaws of death, was not vouchsafed;—and late on that unhappy Christmas Day, the child breathed its last in Emily's embrace.

When the sad tidings were communicated to Lorimer, who was in another room, he repaired to the chamber in which the corpse lay; and he affected to weep over that pale lily so early cropped from the crowded garden of the human race. But suddenly he was startled by a reminiscence which smote him as a pang: for had not the wronged and betrayed Margaret bade him beware of the incidents which occurred on a Christmas Day?—and was this child's death by some means so inscrutably connected with his own destiny, that it was to exercise an influence upon the future circumstances of his life? The thought was for a moment overpowering; and Emily, who witnessed his emotion, fancied that he was cruelly shocked by Isabella's departure from this world. Nor did he undeceive her: but endeavouring to banish his gloomy ideas, he quitted the chamber.

He was descending the stairs, which were lighted only by the pale moonbeams that shone through the casement upon the landing, when a soft but sweet strain of music appeared suddenly to fill the air around him,—so gentle and low that it might be assimilated to that perpetuation of melodious sounds in the ears which one experiences after quitting a concert-room where the harmony has just ceased. It was some moments before it found its way from Lorimer's ear to his mind, so full of thought was the latter: but when he became aware that it was stealing over him, like a mysterious influence which he *felt* rather than a melody which he *heard*, he paused—trembled—and leant against the wall for support. For nearly a minute did he thus listen—his attention being rivetted in spite of himself: then, suddenly pressing his hand violently against his brow, he endeavoured to persuade himself that it was nothing more than the freak of a disordered fancy, and continued to descend the stairs. But still the harmony stole upon his sense— low, plaintive, and tender, but exquisitely sweet;—

G

while a few paces in advance of him, the moonbeams appeared to be playing with a more than
usual brilliancy, as if concentrating all their silver
radiance in one spot. His eyes were fixed upon this
phenomenon, as his ears were already enchained by
that mysterious music; and the idea gradually
strengthened in his mind that the moonbeams were
taking the shape of a small and delicate, but perfect
human figure. Again he paused in dismay—and behold! at the foot of the stairs he beheld the radiant
form of a young child, quite naked, and transparent as if it were a mere embodiment of that light
which the moon and stars send forth. Yet so full
of intelligence were the features of the infant, that
the conscience-stricken Lorimer could read upon its
countenance an expression of such profound melancholy mingled with so much plaintive reproach, that
to his startled soul rushed all that the dying Margaret had uttered in respect to the fate of young
children who perished unbaptized! He was about
to give vent to a cry of terror, when the vision
began rapidly to fade away, the music growing

fainter and fainter at the same time;—and as the celestial melody died upon the sense which it had enthralled, the apparition melted into air.

For several minutes Lorimer remained rooted to the spot, stupified—paralysed—with the blood frozen in his veins. All the misdeeds of the last few years of his life appeared to be proclaiming themselves with a thousand mysterious tongues around him. But his mind, naturally endowed with a vigour that does not characterise ordinary mortals, at length began to recover from this appalling consternation; and, with almost a superhuman effort, he shook off the superstitious influence that had seized upon him. Descending to the parlour, he filled a tumbler with strong wine which he drank at a draught; and it went hissing down his parched throat as if streaming over red-hot iron. He then threw himself on a sofa and began to reason upon the phenomena which he had heard and witnessed; until he arrived at the conclusion that the fact of the child's death, the remorse which had stricken him on account of having broken his solemn pledge to have it baptized, and the remembrance of the wild legend which a dying woman had breathed in his ears, had so operated upon his mind as to render it temporarily susceptible of a superstitious influence. But in order to assure himself that there was nothing real in the music,—and if that were a freak of fancy, the apparition might be looked upon as equally ideal,—he retraced his way to the chamber of death, under pretence of consoling his wife. He remained there for several minutes; and as she said nothing to him respecting the mysterious melody, he was now fully convinced that all the sources of his alarm were to be attributed to a disordered imagination.

In the course of two or three days the impression which had been made upon Lorimer's mind died away; and when the corpse of the unbaptized Isabella was deposited in the earth, he almost ceased to remember the incidents which, whether real or imaginary, had so much alarmed him in the evening of Christmas Day. Weeks and months rolled on; and Emily's grief for the loss of Isabella became first mellowed down into a pious resignation, and was ultimately absorbed in the tenderness which she lavished upon her own little Arthur, who throve apace. But by the time he was eighteen months old, he began to manifest, in those minute but significant phases of the disposition which the eye of a mother can read so truly and so soon, the impatience and self-will which, in the matured development of his father's character, had become a habit of imperious command and a haughty repugnance to anything like contradiction. His features, also, bore in miniature the impress of his sire's energetic and severe countenance; and yet, for all this, Emily loved the boy the more—because, whatever Lorimer might be to the rest of the world, he was not unkind nor harsh towards her.

The year 1790 was drawing to a close; and another Christmas Day came. There was no illness in the lawyer's dwelling now: the events of the preceding anniversary of the Saviour's birth were almost obliterated from his mind;—and after a long season of close application to his business and to his law studies, did he hail this day of perfect rest. In the morning he accompanied his wife to the parish church; and, when the service was over, she besought him to pass by that spot where the remains of Isabella lay deep beneath the turf of the cemetery. He complied with this request; and, although for a few minutes the contemplation of the little grave drew tears from Emily's eyes, she afterwards felt relieved as if she had performed a duty. But although Lorimer had just beheld not only the resting-place of *his own child*, but likewise that of the wronged and heart-broken Margaret, his obdurate nature was not moved by a tender feeling, even if it were for a moment accessible to the slightest remorse.

On regaining the villa Lorimer and his wife were met on the threshold by little Arthur, who was now nearly twenty months old, and who came bounding with outstretched arms and joyous shouts, towards them. The fond mother caught him to her bosom and covered him with kisses: for she thought how unhappy she should be were the same premature fate which had borne Isabella to the tomb, to overtake her own well-beloved darling.

The dinner-hour arrived; and little Arthur occupied a high chair by Emily's side. Need we say that the good old Christmas fare appeared upon the board,—that the turkey was one of the finest which Devonshire could produce, or that the pudding was compounded after the most approved receipt? Mr. Lorimer was in excellent spirits; and, in a humour of more than usual communicativeness towards his wife, he intimated to her the serious thoughts that he had for some time entertained of removing to London and studying for the bar. He declared that he was growing impatient of the narrow sphere to which his energies and his capacities were confined in that secluded town; and that he had imbibed a strong distaste for the profession of a simple attorney. Animated with a glass or two of wine, he shadowed forth the ambitious views which he entertained, and prophesied an almost incalculable success were he to become a member of the bar, with the extensive field of Westminster Hall to allow full play to those intellectual powers which he knew himself to possess. Emily listened with attention and delight: for, although she loved the villa and the retirement in which they dwelt, yet her affections were so completely devoted to her husband that his wishes became her own the instant they were expressed.

While they were thus conversing, little Arthur had been put down from his chair, and had played about the room. Presently a maid-servant, who entered the room for some purpose, inadvertently left the door open ; and the child went out into the passage. The incident was unnoticed by either Lorimer or his wife for perhaps ten minutes or a quarter of an hour: and when Emily looked round, and missed the little fellow, she immediately fancied that the domestic had taken him with her. But as the door was open, and a cutting draught swept into the dining-room, she rose to shut it : when, feeling the wind to be entering the house with chilling effect, she looked out and noticed that the back door was standing wide open. Lorimer, who was in an excellent humour, as we have already stated, and who was gratified by the manner in which his wife had met the proposal relative to a removal to London, instantly volunteered to shut the obnoxious door ; and, Emily returning to her seat, he quitted the room.

The back-door alluded to opened upon the garden; and when Lorimer reached the threshold, he paused for a few moments to cool his brow, which an extra glass of wine (for he was habitually very temperate) and the excitement of the recent conversation had flushed and heated. But scarcely had he taken his stand there and looked forth into the pure, frosty, and moon-lit evening, when his ears became sensible of a soft, plaintive, and sweetly beautiful strain of music stealing upon them; and at the same instant he beheld the moonbeams concentrating, as it were, in the middle of the garden. An icy tremor came over him: but he was rivetted to the spot—his lips were sealed,—he could neither move nor cry out. The dulcet melody continued—and the shape of the radiant infant once more appeared before his eyes,

with its softly melancholy and reproachful countenance turned towards him.   Was this again a delusion?   He asked himself the question: but he had
not time to reason upon the answer, ere he beheld
his little son bound along the pathway towards the
phenomenon of the transparent child of light,—
clapping his tiny hands and shouting for joy.   For
the boy had strayed into the garden, the back-door
being left open; and, although so young, he had not
felt afraid in the semi-obscurity of the evening—
but had rather delighted in the enjoyment of this
freedom.

A terrible sensation of increased terror—a pre-
sentiment that something dreadful was about to
happen — seized upon Lorimer, as he thus beheld
Arthur approach the radiant child : and yet the
unhappy father was still held motionless—powerless
—silent, as if a magic spell were upon him.   But
what pen can describe the agony which rent his
heart, when he saw the apparition move rapidly
along the garden towards the picturesque bridge
that crossed the stream skirting the enclosure in

that direction,—while his son followed the pixy with a speed that seemed marvellous for a child not quite twenty months old! At the same time the plaintive music grew fainter and fainter as if retreating along with the radiant infant; and, though the wretched lawyer was racked by feelings of excruciating poignancy, he was still rivetted statue-like, and as a statue voiceless, to the spot. In a few moments the pixy gained the bridge—and traversed it, little Arthur still following;—and when the stream was crossed by the supernatural guide and its pursuer, Lorimer fell forward insensible upon the ground.

When consciousness returned, he was in bed—and candles were burning upon the table: but the curtain was drawn so as to veil the light from his eyes. He did not speak immediately—nor did he even by a movement give intimation that he had awakened to life again. For his first thoughts were that something dreadful had happened, although he could not recollect what it was: but by degrees his ideas grew settled—the terrible incidents of the evening rose, like a slow and awful phantasmagoria, to his memory—and in a few minutes he comprehended all that had occurred. But could it have been a delusion?—or was it a shocking reality? Had his son been spirited away by a pixy? He would ascertain if Arthur were safe in the house—and, if so, he might still persuade himself that he had merely been passing through another phase of a fancy periodically disordered. But, ah! his forehead was wrapped round with linen—and his left arm was likewise bandaged: it was true, then, that he had fallen—that he had hurt his head—and that he had been bled! Yes—and still that fall might have been occasioned by a fit? Hark! what are those sounds which meet his ear? They are sobs,—deep, profound, suffocating sobs — indicative of a dreadful grief. Unable to endure the tortures of suspense any longer, the attorney drew aside the curtain; and Emily, starting from a chair, threw herself upon his breast, weeping bitterly—bitterly!

For a long time the silence remained unbroken, save by the convulsive anguish of the young wife;—and Lorimer felt—keenly felt the conviction steal into his soul that his son was lost. Emily would not be thus distracted, were it otherwise: she would rejoice that *he* had awakened to consciousness and life. These reflections passed through his brain with the vivid rapidity of lightning;—and now he nerved himself for an awful struggle with his feelings. He dared not reveal what he had witnessed in the garden: he must affect to be ignorant of little Arthur's disappearance until the intelligence should fall from his wife's lips. Oh! the tremendous hypocrisy of which this man was capable!

But some minutes elapsed ere he could induce his tongue to frame the question which he knew was to elicit a reply that would not leave the shadow of a hope behind. At length he did murmur forth a few words, beseeching Emily not to weep for *his* sake;—adding that "it was a vertigo—a sudden fit—perhaps a slight touch of apoplexy—but he felt that all danger was over now."

"Oh! how can I tell you what has occurred!" exclaimed the wretched woman, almost frantic with grief. " Arthur — our darling Arthur — our

H

cherished, beloved boy——O God! have mercy upon me!"—and, falling back upon the chair again, she gave vent to an anguish beyond all power of imagining.

Lorimer now put rapid and apparently anxious questions; and when at last he received the dreaded, but foreknown answer, and learnt that his son—his well-beloved son—was indeed snatched from him, he was afforded an opportunity of yielding to all the affliction that had hitherto remained pent-up and subdued in the depths of his soul.

It appeared that Mrs. Lorimer, wondering why he did not return to the parlour, and still feeling the draught of the open door, had gone forth at the expiration of ten minutes for the purpose of seeking him; when, to her horror, she found him stretched lifeless upon the threshold. To summon the servants —have him conveyed up-stairs—and to send for medical assistance, were her first impulses; and when the doctor came, he at once declared that Mr. Lorimer had been attacked by a severe fit. He was bled in the arm—and the wound which he had received on the forehead was dressed; and it was not until all this was over, that little Arthur was missed. Then how terrific were the apprehensions which seized upon the unhappy mother!—what could have become of him? That he had strayed through the open door into the garden, was evident; and when it was discovered that the gate on the bridge was likewise open, the worst fears were entertained. Nevertheless, he could not have been drowned in the stream, because it was frozen over and the surface was unbroken. Had he, then, been stolen? The thought was anguish —it was like dropping molten lead upon the brain laid bare. The two servants were despatched in search of the child: the doctor volunteered to undertake the same task,— and Emily—the wretched Emily—was left alone in the house to watch by the side of her husband. But not for an instant did the unhappy lady associate the sudden fit which had stricken him, with the disappearance of the boy: on the contrary, she imagined that Arthur must have strayed away during the confusion which followed the discovery of Mr.

Lorimer lying senseless across the threshold of the door.

Two hours had elapsed since that incident when the patient awoke in the manner already described. Presently one of the servants returned—exhausted with a vain ramble in every direction. Soon afterwards, the other came back from an equally unsuccessful search;—and last of all the doctor made his appearance, having been unable to glean the slightest trace of the lost child. Poor Emily was almost heart-broken: but we can find no words to convey an adequate idea of her bitter—bitter affliction.

As for Lorimer—his was a state of mind which the criminal about to be executed would have scarcely envied. His countenance was ghastly pallid—and yet his head was on fire. The sense of desolation that was upon him, appeared to scorch his brain. No tears came now to his glowing eyes: but a pandemonium raged in his heart. O Margaret! thou wast already avenged. Even from the tomb did thine hatred work its effect upon him who

wronged thee!—even from the grave did thy male-
diction pursue the man who suffered thy child, which
was also *his* child, to perish unbaptised! No longer
did the wretched Lorimer doubt the legend which
thy lips breathed as thou didst lie upon the bed of
death: no longer did he disbelieve in the existence
of the pixy. Nor less was his soul opened to the terrible conviction that thou, Margaret! didst utter no
unmeaning thing in the shape of that solemn warning which declared *that the Christian season, to
others a blessing, should be to him a curse!*

But it is not our purpose to dwell upon this portion of our narrative. Suffice it to say that although
neither trouble nor expense was spared in searching
for the lost child,—although printed bills were pro-
fusely circulated throughout the neighbouring districts, offering the reward of five hundred pounds
for the restoration of the boy,—and although emis-
saries were employed to travel about making inquiries in every direction within a circuit of thirty
miles of the town—still not a trace of little Arthur
could be obtained. Many, many months elapsed ere

these attempts to recover him were finally abandoned as hopeless; and when another Christmas Day
arrived, and Lorimer, as he sate down to table with
his wife, beheld the care-worn, wasted, and faded
being that she had become, he could not avert his
mental gaze from contemplating the melancholy
contrast which she presented to the blooming,
beautiful, happy woman who had graced his board a
year ago! And the conscience-stricken man, who
was himself much altered, felt the worm of remorse
gnawing at his heart's core: for he knew that all
the bitter affliction which had entered his house like
a desolating army, was to be traced back to his
broken vow respecting the baptism of Margaret's
child!

Eighteen months after the disappearance of little
Arthur, Mr. and Mrs. Lorimer removed to London,
where the attorney entered himself as a student for
the bar. He took a fine house in a fashionable
square—furnished it splendidly—and courted the
most brilliant society of the metropolis. Emily
wondered whence came all the money that enabled

her husband to launch out in such an expensive mode of life: but she never asked him for any explanation. She presided at the table to which noble guests were invited—appeared in her drawing-rooms which were thronged with high-born ladies—and rode in the carriage that was provided for her use. All this she did to please him whom she loved, and whose slightest wish was still her law: but a smile never shone upon her pale and melancholy countenance—and in the midst of gaiety she was as sad as a hopeless affliction could render her.

CHAPTER V.

THE SPY.

TWENTY years had passed away since the Lorimers arrived in London,—twenty long years, during which nations had beheld and undergone such vast and so many changes. Oh! let fancy plume her wings beyond the flight of Time, and she shall imagine no era of the world's history more strange—more wonderful than the period which embraced those twenty years. The French Revolution had shattered to pieces a throne whereon forty Kings had in succession sate,—Corsica had sent forth that meteor-man whose glory astonished the whole earth with its dazzling lustre, and who had placed an imperial diadem upon his brow,—corporals had risen

to be Princes, Dukes, and Marshals,—and the unknown individuals of yesterday had become crowned
monarchs to-day!

In England alone had no change comparatively
taken place.   The aristocracy and the wealthy
oligarchy used the whip and spur as heretofore to
goad the toiling millions to slave for them: and those
millions starved that a few thousands might live in
luxurious indolence. Discontent pervaded the manufacturing districts and the rural population : in-
cendiarism rendered night terrible with its lurid
glare;—and meetings of the working classes were
taking place all over the country. At this juncture,
the Ministers were resolved to adopt the usual course
of tyranny : instead of inquiring into the public
grievances with a view of redressing them, they
decided upon making examples! But it was necessary to find a man who would undertake the odious
task of sending into exile or to the gibbet a few
dozens of the discontented mechanics and peasants,
—a man who possessed great legal knowledge, so as
to ferret out at a moment's notice some old and

obsolete Acts of Parliament, under the shadow of which a vile despotism might work out its detestable purposes—a man, in fine, who united transcendent abilities with an utter want of principle. The Ministers looked around them, we say, for such a man: and their eyes settled upon a barrister who had risen rapidly in his profession—whose eloquence was so versatile that at one moment he could thunder and denounce, at another weep and persuade—whose ambition was notorious, whose fortune was princely, and who was already fitted by the training of a couple of sessions in the House of Commons to defend in that assembly all the iniquities which it was now determined to perpetrate under the cover of a judge and jury, and by the aid of the hangman and the transport-ship. This man was Arthur Lorimer: and, behold! the *Gazette* publishes his nomination to the post of Attorney-General, with the honour of Knighthood.

Emily was still alive,—alive in the form of a woman prematurely old—with false locks concealing hair as white as snow, and false teeth as a substitute for the pearls that once appeared between the parting roses of lips now thin and pale.   Such was Lady Lorimer in her fortieth year!   Her husband, now verging close upon fifty, was a tall, stern-looking, severe man, with iron-grey hair encircling a massive head bald upon the crown,—a sallow complexion,— and an expression of countenance one glance at which would freeze upon the lip the appeal that Hope was about to breathe — make justice shrink back in despair—and carry to Mercy's heart the conviction that it were useless to kneel in intercession at *his* feet!

About a fortnight after the accession of Arthur Lorimer to the post of Attorney-General, and on a cold, rainy afternoon in the month of July, 1811, a middle-aged man of repulsive appearance turned from Fleet Street into the Temple.   He was clad almost in the rags of beggary; but there was nevertheless an attempted decency manifest in his attire, which proved that he had known better days.   His coarse features and brutal expression of countenance indicated long years of low debauchery; and in the depths of his small, dark, reptile-like eyes lurked all the ferocity of hardened sin. He was a man who had been almost everything by turns in an irregular way of life,—a bill-discounter, or rather a bill-stealer —a horse-dealer, or more often a horse-chaunter—a gambler, of the species known as "black-leg"—a hanger-on at police-offices and assize-courts, ready to sell his perjury to prove an *alibi* for a prisoner, or as a witness to complete a defective case on the part of a malignant prosecutor—a frequenter of public-house parlours, where he made bets upon points raised by himself and of the issue of which he was assured beforehand—a begging-letter impostor when times went particularly hard with him—a secretary to a loan-society or coal-club, with the proceeds of which he was sure to decamp some fine morning—a periodical visitor to the debtors' prisons of the metropolis, and a frequent applicant to the Insolvents' Court as a natural consequence—a Saint for a season at Exeter Hall,—in fine, one of those locomotive moral pests who live by their wits and who are ready to do anything or everything for money.

Such was the individual, who, now completely broken down and finding all his ingenuity pretty well exhausted, turned into the Temple—proceeded direct to King's Bench Walk — and entered the offices of the Attorney-General. Sir Arthur Lorimer was there at the time and disengaged at the moment: and, after some little hesitation on the part of the clerks to escort such a hang-dog looking fellow into the presence of the great law-officer, he succeeded in obtaining the interview which he so much desired, and on which his last hope appeared to rest.

The moment that this individual stood before the Attorney-General, the latter by a species of intuitive perception conjectured the object of his call : for on what *other* business could a man, whose entire appearance at once indicated the broken-down adventurer, presume to venture thither? But it was not for Sir Arthur Lorimer to show that he had already divined the purport of the visit : and he accordingly demanded in a severe — nay, almost savage tone—what he wanted.

"I should like to help the Government to restore peace and order in the country," answered the man, without taking the trouble to use any circumlocution: "for I am a loyal subject—a sincere believer in the divine right of Kings—a staunch upholder of Church and State—an advocate of capital punishment—a regular Tory—and all that sort of thing."

"Ah! I understand," said the Attorney-General, scrutinizing him with eagle-looks that seemed to pierce him through and through. "What is your name?"

"William Harpinger," was the reply; and the fellow rubbed round his old worn-out beaver with the cuff of his thread-bare black coat.

"But what guarantee can you give that you will serve us faithfully?" demanded Sir Arthur Lorimer.

"Just this," was the ready answer: "that I am pennyless—homeless—friendless—foodless—characterless; and if I don't succeed in getting employment from you, I must go straight off and make a hole in the water. In a word, I will do anything for money."

"So far, so good," observed the cautious Lorimer. "But suppose that we supply you with money for the purpose of going down into the discontented districts, how are we to be assured that you or the cash will ever get farther than the nearest ale-house in Fleet Street?"

"Look here, Sir Arthur," responded Harpinger: "I am tired of being knocked about the world as I have been ever since I was twenty—and I want to get something certain. If I serve you faithfully and effectually, a matter of five hundred pounds or so won't hurt you when it's all over: and therefore I am not likely to lose that sum in anticipation, by cheating you out of a beggarly ten or twenty pound note in the first instance. I'm not quite such a fool as all that, I can tell you. Now do you understand me?"

"Well—I do not think you reason unfairly," said the Attorney-General; "and I am disposed to give you a trial. The fact is," he continued, after a short pause, and sinking his voice to a mysterious whisper, "we *do* require such a man as you. Cases of high treason are difficult of proof, without the aid of—of——"

"Spies and informers," exclaimed Harpinger, bluntly. "Out with it!"

"We will call them *approvers*, my good friend," returned Sir Arthur, now becoming confidential in tone and encouraging in manner: for he foresaw all the *valuable* aid which such a thorough-paced scoundrel as this man, whose character he had read in a few minutes, could render the object which the Government had in view. "But, as I was observing, we *do* need approvers in the present deplorable state of the country—and repugnant as it is to our feelings——"

"This is the first time I ever heard that a Government had any feelings at all," interrupted Harpinger, coarsely. "But go on, Sir Arthur."

"Be your opinion whatever it may," said the Attorney-General, suddenly resuming his freezing coldness of tone, "the Government *has* feelings— and those of the most paternal kind. Is it not for their own good, that we wish to strike terror into the hearts of the disorderly rabbles that are now engaged in tumultuous meetings and seditious designs? Certainly it is, Mr. Harpinger: and if you wish to enter the service of the Government, you must at once adopt the right spirit."

"God bless you, Sir Arthur," exclaimed the man, "I can put on any spirit you like just as easy as a glove. Come, then—I agree to the conditions—and henceforth and for ever I give the Government credit for the best of feelings in this and all other matters."

"Now you acquire my confidence," said Sir Arthur: "for believe me when I assure you that it is with the deepest regret I have accepted the laborious, unthankful, and invidious post which I now occupy; and nothing but an ardent desire to rescue my beloved country from a ruinous anarchy could have induced me to resign my professional independence for the trammels of office. Remember, then, Mr. Harpinger, that *you* have not embraced the position of approver for the sake of money— neither have you any ulterior object in view. You are not animated by a desire of recompense—nor do you expect it. Nor are you even now paid by the Government: because if I presently place a fifty-pound note upon the table and you pocket it slily while I turn my back—and then if I don't miss it afterwards — why, you could safely declare upon oath in a court of justice that you were *not* bribed to take certain steps in a certain matter."

"Ah! now I understand what you are driving at!" exclaimed Harpinger, who at first could not for the life of him conceive why the Attorney-General should launch forth into all that bombast about the paternal feelings of the Government—his own pure and patriotic motives in taking office—and the proper spirit which must animate those who served the Ministry.

"In a word," continued Sir Arthur Lorimer, "you, Mr. Harpinger, are painfully alive to the necessity of adopting severe measures to suppress discontent and compel the millions to respect the laws; and you are prepared to make any personal sacrifice for the good of your country. You will even incur the odium of becoming an approver; because when all is over, you can lay your hand upon your heart and exclaim proudly, '*At least I have done my duty!*' "

" Upon my soul, sir, you almost melt me to tears," cried Harpinger. " I could not have fancied that I was the disinterested, conscientious, straight-forward man and sincere patriot that you so eloquently represent me to be. But now I feel that I am in reality all you say—and I shall make the best of these amiable qualities."

" I trust you will," observed Sir Arthur Lorimer: then, laying a Bank-note for fifty pounds upon the table, he walked towards the window, observing, " It is very unpleasant weather, Mr. Harpinger."

" Very, sir," responded this individual, as he consigned the note to his pocket, while a grin of satisfaction appeared upon his dissipated countenance. " I think we have nothing more to say to each other *now*—but in a very short time you shall hear from me."

" Good afternoon, Mr. Harpinger," said the great law-officer; and the man took his departure, exulting in the success of his visit, but—villain though he was—loathing the detestable hypocrisy of his employer.

A few days after the interview just related, Mr. Harpinger alighted from the top of a coach in the good city of Exeter. For he had determined to commence proceedings in the county of Devon, which was at that time characterised by an extraordinary degree of fermentation on the part of the labouring classes. The miserable peasantry were ground down to the very dust by the tyrannical landowners: the immense pressure of taxation, arising from the iniquitous wars into which England had so madly plunged for the sake of the Spanish Bourbons, was felt to the very lowest grades of society;—prices were high and provisions were scarce; and the greater became the grievances of the people, the more insolent grew the aristocracy. In all the districts around Exeter, the agricultural labourers were starving; and the wan features of their sickly children presented the unmistakable marks of famine. A few days' rambling amongst the peasantry convinced Harpinger of these facts; and he speedily ascertained that secret meetings were being held and unions formed for the purpose of adopting measures to compel the landlords to yield to the just demands made upon them in respect to wages.

Harpinger threw himself in the way of the leaders of these associations — conversed with them upon their wrongs — expatiated upon the selfishness and despotism of the lords of the soil—and so worked upon the feelings of his listeners that they panted for revenge. He insinuated himself into their confidence, and by pretending to reveal to them his own secrets, elicited theirs. By degrees he darkly hinted that he was an emissary sent from the manufacturing districts in the north to sound the disposition of the people in the south; and, on another occasion speaking more openly, he exhibited forged credentials which at once averted suspicion, even if any were for a moment entertained. He then stated that the men of Manchester, Liverpool, Leeds, and Birmingham were ready to rise: and he gave such a glowing picture of the enthusiasm which inspired the work-

ing classes in those great towns, that the persons to
whom he thus spoke with a rough but fervid eloquence, began to be ashamed of themselves for the
little progress they had made in their preparations
to resist the law. They therefore naturally applied
to Harpinger for his counsel and assistance; and, as
a necessary preliminary, he was installed a member
of the leading secret committee, which held its
meetings at a way-side public-house about twenty-
five miles from Exeter. He at once recommended
that money should be raised to purchase arms; and,
throwing open his coat, he convinced his audience
that he himself had already set the example. His
advice was adopted; subscriptions were opened
accordingly,—and he was solicited to contract with
some house at Birmingham for the supply. In fact,
so zealous did he appear in the people's cause—so
uncompromising an enemy did he proclaim himself
to all existing institutions — and so well did his
rugged eloquence work with those to whose minds
it was addressed, that he gained the most complete
influence over the committee.

Thus did several weeks pass away; and frequent
were the communications made by the spy to the
Attorney-General in London. Money was remitted
to him from time to time ; but no *written* instructions were ever sent. But on one occasion some
individual—whom he thought he remembered to
have seen at the clerk's desk in Sir Arthur Lorimer's
office in the Temple—came down to Exeter to see
him, and intimated that, as a great amount of dis-
affection was understood to exist among the small
farmers in Devonshire, he must keep his eye upon
that class as well as on the operatives themselves.
Harpinger understood the hint : the Government
wanted to make an example of a man of some standing, in addition to the "rabble" for whom it was
thus setting its snares;—and the villanous spy was
resolved that this new aim should be accomplished.
By the means of information which he had at his
command, through the members of the secret committee and other malcontents, he learnt all the particulars he required with respect to the position,
character, and opinions of the principal small

farmers within a circuit of thirty miles of Exeter; and he had now only to look around him and select his *victim!*

His choice fell upon a young man, of remarkably handsome person, good disposition, and industrious habits. His name was Albert Langdon; and he rented a small farm at a distance of about ten or a dozen miles from Exeter. He was married to an excellent young woman, of great beauty, and who was of his own age, which was about three-and-twenty. They had been united for nearly a year, having loved each other even from their very child-hood: for they had been brought up together. They were a superior couple for their class of life, unusual care having been bestowed upon their edu-cation: and in his leisure hours Albert was fond of reading instructive books to his beloved wife, while she was occupied with her needle. Their position was a comfortable one in all respects: for they had commenced farming and housekeeping with a good supply of ready money, as the young woman's parents were in very respectable circumstances and

K

had a freehold of some extent in the vicinity of Exeter.

Situated as Albert Langdon was, it may seem strange that Harpinger should have chosen him as his intended victim—especially as the youthful farmer was not connected with the movement then in progress. But he had been heard to express an opinion in its favour, and to declare that his sympathies were entirely on the side of the operatives. Moreover, his disposition was liberal, and his soul was animated with a fervour and endowed with a strength of feeling well calculated to render him enthusiastic in any cause which he might embrace. It was therefore a knowledge of these features in his character which induced Harpinger to fix his eyes upon him.

To obtain an introduction to a small farmer in a county famed for the hospitality of its inhabitants, was no difficult matter; and Harpinger, by his conversational powers, a judicious use of the varied information which he had picked up in the course of his chequered life, and that appearance of frankness and sincerity, amounting at times to bluntness, which he knew so well how to assume and which fitted him so admirably for the detestable part which he was playing,—by means of all these qualifications we say, Harpinger was enabled to gain the esteem and confidence of the young man. He however saw that from the very first he was no favourite with Mrs. Langdon; and he therefore speedily refrained from visiting at their abode. But he sought out Albert in the fields; and, drawing him insensibly into political discussions, argued with such seeming fervour upon the wrongs sustained by the agricultural classes, that he soon found a willing listener in the young man. Albert grew discontented: the poison was working in his veins—and, although he concealed from his wife the new ideas which had sprung up within him, he nevertheless pondered on them profoundly when alone. But it would occupy pages to describe how Harpinger worked upon the feelings of the enthusiatic Albert: for although the miscreant told him nothing that was untrue, when he expatiated upon the oppressed condition of the

tolling millions in this country—yet he *did* lavish
innumerable falsehoods when he represented the im-
minence of a well-organised rebellion, and spoke of
the readiness of all the great towns and most popu-
lous districts to strike a blow for their rights.   In a
word, Albert Langdon consented to accompany
Harpinger to a meeting of the secret committee,
merely to listen to the speakers and obtain a better
insight into the aims and objects of the association.

It was upon this night that Harpinger delivered
to the assembly a quantity of arms which had just
arrived from Birmingham;—and when a pair of
pistols was thrust upon Albert, he scarcely knew how
to refuse the gift.   Nevertheless, he *did* hesitate; but
when Harpinger whispered to him that he would be
taken for a spy if he acted differently from the rest,
he coloured with indignation at the bare idea of in-
curring such an ignominious suspicion, and secured
the weapons about his person.   The deliberations
commenced; and Harpinger made a most exciting
speech, urging the committee to delay active proceedings no longer, as the men of Lancashire and

Warwickshire intended to rise simultaneously on the following night; and he advised an attack to be made upon Exeter at the same time. Never was his eloquence so powerful—never did he seem more sternly resolved and honestly sincere. His listeners were electrified;—and even Albert Langdon himself was profoundly moved, although he was very far from being prepared to go to any such length as that recommended. But, to his surprise and dismay, the proposal was embodied in a resolution which was put from the chair; and every hand save his own was held up in its favour. Then again did the fatal—terrible whisper sound in his ears, that he would be looked upon as a spy if he were found to be the only dissentient;—and, in a moment of delirium—while his brain was in a whirl—he raised his hand!

Almost immediately afterwards the room in the public-house where the meeting took place, was invaded by soldiers with their bayonets fixed; and although in the desperate struggle which ensued, several of the members contrived to effect their escape—amongst whom was Harpinger—yet five were taken prisoners.

And the unfortunate Albert Langdon was of the number!

CHAPTER VI.

THE TRIAL.

In the month of December, of the same year, a special commission issued for the trial of the Devonshire prisoners on a charge of high treason; and great was the excitement which prevailed at Exeter as the time approached for the judicial proceedings. Two Judges, notoriously the most rancorous Tories that sate upon the bench, were appointed to preside; and the Attorney-General, Sir Arthur Lorimer, was to prosecute. It was not however known, until the commission was gazetted, that the prisoners were to be tried for the most serious offence of which the law takes cognizance; the general impression since their arrest having been that they would be accused of secret assembling, with arms, for seditious purposes. But on the eve of the proceedings it was whispered for the first time that an individual named Harpinger would give evidence as an approver for the Government!

The Judges, the Attorney-General, and several eminent barristers arrived at Exeter on the 16th of December; and at nine o'clock on the following morning the special commission was opened. The court was crowded to suffocation: for not only had the serious nature of the charge against the prisoners produced the greatest excitement throughout the city and the surrounding districts, but the most lively interest was felt on behalf of *one*, who from his youth and previous character enlisted sentiments of profound commiseration in his favour. There was also a deep curiosity experienced to hear the Attorney-General, whose eloquence was said to transcend any specimens of forensic oratory, whether ancient or modern, and who now sate at the table with a countenance more severe and implacable than it perhaps had ever seemed before.

The Judges entered the court: silence was proclaimed—and the senior functionary began to charge
the Grand Jury. It must have appeared strange to
the ears of the thinking portion of the audience to
mark how he was compelled to travel back, through
the long vista of years, into remote semi-barbarian
ages, in order to drag forth from those times of
darkness and obscurity the old statutes on which the
law of treason was based,—strange also to hear how
he dwelt upon the precedents furnished by far-
distant periods when our ancestors, whose "wisdom"
is so much vaunted, believed in necromancy and
burnt witches,—and stranger still to observe how he
applied those cases belonging to epochs of a blood-
thirsty despotism, to a century of civilisation and
progress. In fact, his charge was a tremendous
piece of special pleading against the prisoners; and
the Grand Jury returned true bills accordingly.

Albert Langdon was then ordered to be placed in
the dock; and presently the Bench and the Bar
beheld a tall, genteel, dark-eyed, and handsome
young man ascend into the ominous place with a

firm step. His countenance was very pale; and the
moment he entered the court, he cast his looks
anxiously around. But *those* whose glances he
feared to meet, were not to be seen: they had faithfully kept a promise which he had exacted from
them on the preceding day, and which was to the
effect that they would not be present at the trial—
for he dreaded lest their grief should unman him.
Need we declare that it was his beloved wife and her
revered parents to whom we thus allude?

An able barrister had been retained for the
defence of the unhappy young man; and the swear-
ing in of the petty jury commenced. Now, if there
were any intention to afford Albert Langdon a fair
trial, and if there were no attempt on the part of
the Attorney-General to pack a panel suited to his
interests, why did this great functionary strain every
nerve and avail himself of every means within his
reach to render the prisoner's right of challenge a
mere nullity? Yet such was the conduct of Sir
Arthur Lorimer; and he fully succeeded in his aim.

He then rose to open the case for the prosecution.

All the powers of a colossal intellect—all the fervour
of a brilliant eloquence—and all the profound legal
knowledge that bore upon the case, were called into
request by the Attorney-General on this occasion.
Had he been pleading for his own life instead of
against that of the prisoner, he could not have made
more gigantic efforts to accomplish his purpose. It
seemed as if his honour—his fortune—his very existence depended upon the verdict which he sought to
wring from the jury: it appeared as if he himself
would be doomed to perdition if he failed in sending
that young man to the scaffold. Never were twelve
men so ardently implored—so persuasively besought
—so earnestly prayed to yield up to the executioner
the life of a fellow-creature. One would have thought
that the annihilation of the whole human race,—or
at least some frightful national calamity,—would be
inevitable, were Albert Langdon to be acquitted.
At length the speech, which occupied six hours, was
terminated with a magnificent peroration; and, as if
to impart the fullest effect to his fervid eloquence,
Sir Arthur Lorimer sank down into his seat with

well-assumed exhaustion, as the last words fell from
his tongue. The Court then adjourned until the
next morning; and the spectators dispersed in
silence, shaking their heads gloomily.

On the following day, Harpinger was placed in
the witness-box; and he met with a cool indifference
the steadfast but reproachful gaze which Albert bent
upon him. The reader can imagine the nature of
the testimony which he gave; and, when cross-
examined, he was compelled to admit that he had
not only instigated the prisoner to join the secret
meeting, but that he had likewise persuaded the
members thereof by lying reports to resolve upon
measures which at the commencement of their
organization they had never dreamt of. In fact, it
was proved by his own admissions that his intrigues
had converted into a political conspiracy a movement
which was at first nothing more than a combination
against the tyranny of local landlords. And never
was the interference of the Judges more flagrantly
shown at any trial than on this: never was partiality
more indecently manifested. The Attorney-General

objected to innumerable legitimate questions which were put by the prisoner's counsel; and the Court invariably ruled in his favour. So far from the proceedings having the air of a candid and honest endeavour to arrive at the real truth, they seemed to have in constant view the blinking of that truth so far as it told in favour of Albert Langdon. The barrister retained on his behalf, fought nobly against Sir Arthur Lorimer: but at every step he found himself opposed, snubbed, thwarted, and even insulted by the partizan Judges who sate upon the bench.

The case for the prosecution terminated; and the speech for the defence began. But before the able counsel had proceeded many minutes, he was interrupted by the Attorney-General; and in less than a quarter of an hour he was called to order by the Judges. He went on again: but what with the protesting of Sir Arthur Lorimer at one moment, and the interference of the Bench at another, the effect of his oration was completely marred;—he grew dispirited —the brow-beating on the part of the

Judges increased in proportion—the jury manifested signs of fatigue—and the junior counsel on the side of the Crown affected to yawn, thinking that by so doing they would please the Attorney-General. The prisoner's counsel was accordingly bullied and badgered into winding up sooner than he had intended; and a few witnesses having been examined as to character, Sir Arthur Lorimer rose to reply. Again did he beg and implore that young man's death: again did he appeal to all those passions, and feelings, and selfish interests which his stupendous eloquence was so well calculated to excite on the part of the jury;—and when he sate down, it was easy to perceive how the result must inevitably be.

The chief Judge now summed up, carefully dwelling upon any point that told against the prisoner—glossing over every incident that spoke in his favour—and concluding by plainly, openly, and undisguisedly instructing the jury how they were to decide. Then the twelve arbiters of life and death quitted the box; and when they had retired to their own room, the foreman rubbed his hands together in a gleesome manner at the idea of having reached the end of the proceedings, exclaiming in a pleasant and almost jocular tone, " Well, gentlemen —are we agreed? *My* dinner is waiting for me, I know; and I suppose all *yours* are also. We don't want to be locked-up another night—eh? What shall we say, then? *Guilty*." And the remaining eleven, who were as thorough-paced old Tories as the foreman himself, expressed their unanimity in the proposed verdict. They however stayed in the room to chat upon various subjects for about twenty minutes, so as to have the appearance of deliberating maturely on their decision: and then, assuming the most demure physiognomies possible, they returned to the box with the solemn slowness of a funeral procession. In a few moments more the terrible word — " GUILTY" — was pronounced; and a gleam of satisfaction appeared on the countenance of Sir Arthur Lorimer: for he felt that he had triumphed on behalf of the Government—and, as his thoughts rapidly penetrated the vista of unborn years, he beheld the post of Lord High Chancellor awaiting him in the distance. But the prisoner, exercising an almost superhuman command over his own feelings, maintained a rigid firmness of de-meanour which some few present considered to be a brazen hardihood, but which the great majority knew to be the sure and certain sign of conscious in-nocence.

The Judges put on their black caps; and the pre-siding functionary, having delivered himself of a long hypocrital harangue, wound up by passing that bar-barian, revolting, and abhorrent sentence which would excite indignation and disgust even amidst a tribe of South Sea Cannibals. But the old Judge's blood curdled not in his veins—nor did his heart sicken—nor did he loath himself, as he said, "*The awful sentence of the law is, that you, Albert Lang-don, be taken hence to the place whence you came, and be thence drawn on a hurdle to the place of exe-cution; and that you be there hanged by the neck until you are dead; and that afterwards your head shall be severed from your body, and your body shall be divided into four quarters, to be disposed of as his Majesty shall think fit. And may the Lord have mercy upon your soul!"*

The fiend-like judgment was passed—the prisoner was removed—the Judges quitted the bench—the counsel took up their bags to leave the Court—and the crowds poured forth in solemn silence, their blood chilled by the savage atrocity of the sentence. For they—the working-classes—reflected that they were living in a Christian country; and it horrified them to think that *they* shared in the degradation, the shame, and the scandal which such sanguinary ideas and revolting language, when emanating from the tribunal of justice, entailed upon the whole British community.

The trials of the remaining prisoners occupied the three following days: Harpinger appeared as the Government witness, and Sir Arthur Lorimer as the Government prosecutor;—and the proceedings ended in the conviction of the unfortunate wretches and their condemnation to death in the same inhuman terms as those already recorded.

CHAPTER VII.

THE LAST APPEARANCE OF THE PIXY.

It was Christmas Day, 1811; and festivity prevailed in all the mansions of Grosvenor Square save *one*. This was the splendid abode of Sir Arthur and Lady Lorimer; and the anniversary of the Saviour's birth was invariably a period of gloom and mournfulness with them. For it was on a Christmas Day that Emily's little charge, Isabella Jocelyn, had been snatched from her by the rude hand of Death: and it was also on a Christmas Day that her own son was lost—to *her* so unaccountably! Years—long years had passed since then: but when the December season brought round the day on which so many hearts rejoiced, the bereaved mother felt all her grief renewed with an intensity as poignant as when the fearful intelligence first met her ears that her darling Arthur had strayed and was not to be found.

And Lorimer—did he experience a sorrow equally acute? Oh! yes—and far more bitter still, because it was mingled with a remorse for which Time had no healing influence, Wealth no soothing power, and gratified Ambition no balm! To him, also, was Christmas Day a day of horror and alarm : for, with a never-failing regularity, did the soft, plaintive, and mysterious music begin to steal upon his ears as the clock struck nine in the evening of the twenty-fifth of December;—and, while that harmony enveloped him with its superhuman influence, the radiant pixy was wont to appear and bend its melancholy looks on the conscience-stricken man. Vainly had he sought to avoid the dread visitation. On one occasion, as the fatal moment approached, he pleaded indisposition and rushed into the open streets for fresh air: but, as the hour of nine was proclaimed from the thousand churches of tho

mighty Babylon, the music stole on his ears and
the luminous spirit came. On another Christmas
Day, he invited numerous guests, with the pretext
that their presence would enliven his unhappy
Emily: but as the time-piece struck the fatal hour,
the melody began to fill the perfumed atmosphere
of the apartment; and the radiant child rose into a
bright but evanescent existence before his eyes.
Yet none heard the melody nor beheld the apparition, save himself!

Convinced that no expedient could charm away a
periodical visitation which had thus become a portion of his destiny, the unhappy man resigned himself
to the necessity of encountering the reproachful
gaze of the unbaptized child once in every year;—
but as the fatal hour approached, he sought some
pretext to quit the room where his wife sate, and
retire to another apartment from which the groans
that remorse wrung from his tortured soul could
penetrate to no human ear. Thus, while the rich,
talented, and honoured Arthur Lorimer was the
envy of thousands, in his heart was gnawing the

deathless worm, and was burning the unquenchable fire!

But to resume the thread of our narrative. It was, as we have stated at the opening of the chapter, Christmas Day, 1811. Sir Arthur Lorimer had returned from Exeter; and we now behold him sitting down with his wife to a table magnificently spread with all the luxuries of the season. The chandeliers diffused a flood of golden light throughout the room: a cheerful fire blazed in the grate;—and footmen, in sumptuous liveries, were in attendance. But what a mockery was this Christmas banquet for that guilty man and that unhappy lady! It was a cold—a chilling ceremony that they went through for the sake of appearances; and the costly meal was almost untasted. Few were the words that passed between them: a smile never once appeared upon the lips of either;—and when the formal ordeal was over and the servants had retired, they dreaded to be alone together. For the heart of the mother was full of woe—and the heart of the father was full of bitter regrets. On either side conversation was impossible: if they broke the awful silence, they dared not speak of their lost son—and how could they utter a word without alluding to their sad bereavement?

As nine o'clock approached, Sir Arthur Lorimer grew uneasy and restless. His wife observed his darkening mood: but she said nothing. She imagined that the advance of the hour at which their boy was lost twenty-one years back, brought to his soul the harrowing reminiscences of that fatal event: and she could not offer to comfort him—for she, alas! stood in such need of solace! He rose from his seat —muttered some excuse—and quitted the room. Lady Lorimer sought not to detain him : but the instant the door had closed behind him, she covered her thin face with her emaciated hands and burst into a flood of burning—scalding tears!

The Attorney-General hurried to his library, and threw himself on a sofa. His countenance was ghastly pale: his heart was racked with the most torturing sensations. Never—never had he experienced so much dread of the fatal hour as on this occasion. There was a hurry in his brain: his pulse throbbed violently—an awful terror was upon him—and his large dark eyes glared wildly. He looked at his watch: it wanted five minutes to nine. Oh! could he endure those five centuries of indescribable agony?

Some one knocked at the door of the library. Who dared thus to intrude upon his privacy? In an impatient tone he bade the person enter: and a foot-man appeared.

"An elderly man and two women beseech an interview with you, sir," said the domestic. "I re-presented to them that this was not a day nor an hour——"

"Who are these people?" demanded Lorimer sharply.

"The man says that you will perhaps remember the name of Doyle, sir," replied the servant. "They are from Exeter——"

Yes—I recollect it well," observed Sir Arthur. "But what can they want with me? Tell them to call to-morrow morning:"—and he waved the man imperiously away, for the clock in the library was beginning to strike nine.

The door closed;—and now the music was already stealing on his ear,—plaintive, sweet, and low. It seemed as if the very air had become melodious—as if the atmosphere were imbued with a delicious and supernatural harmony. Rivetted to the spot where he was standing when the domestic quitted the room, Sir Arthur Lorimer was like a being suddenly changed into a statue while under the influence of horrified emotions: for the terrible nature of his thoughts had congealed into an appalling expression of countenance. The music continued—wafting its dulcet though mournful strain to his ears; and in a short time a faint lustre, as if some straggling moonbeams had pierced through the thick curtains into the library, began to play—and then to concentrate at the farther extremity of the apartment. The eyes of the Attorney-General were irresistibly fixed upon that spot; and, by degrees, the silvery lustre assumed the shape of the radiant child. But, oh! far more profoundly mournful, and far more

M

touchingly reproachful than ever was now the look
which the spirit of the Unbaptized One bent on Sir
Arthur Lorimer: and his conscience was stricken
with even a more rending pang than he had yet experienced on any previous occasion.

But while this strange and wondrous scene was
yet passing,—and ere the luminous apparition had
begun to melt away, or the music to flow less au-
dibly on his ears,—voices and footsteps in the passage outside were heard: the door was thrown open
—and Lady Lorimer exclaimed, " Yes—enter, good
people! My husband will not refuse to receive you
on such a mournful mission."

At the same instant, the pixy joined its luminous
hands in an appealing manner, and its radiant countenance assumed an expression so touchingly and
eloquently beseeching, that to the soul of Lorimer
flashed the thought that all this must be in some way
connected with the visit of those whom his wife was
just introducing to his presence. The music now
died rapidly away—the spirit of light grew fainter
and fainter; and by the time the persons ushered in

by Lady Lorimer had crossed the threshold of the apartment, the melody had ceased and the pixy had melted into the impalpable air.

The tide of life, which for upwards of a minute had been frozen in the veins of the Attorney-General, now circulated rapidly once again; — and, staggering towards the sofa, the wretched man threw himself thereon.

"Alas! you perceive that my husband has likewise *his* afflictions," said Lady Lorimer to those whom she was escorting; "and he will not therefore turn a deaf ear to the voice of your bitter anguish."

The Attorney-General raised his eyes, and hastily scanned the visitors. The foremost, who was a man bordering upon fifty, had the appearance of being (as he indeed was) a substantial farmer; and his countenance, naturally benevolent in expression, now denoted the workings of a mind wrung with acute suspense. Clinging to his arm was a young woman of about three-and-twenty—very beautiful, but a prey to the most cruel anguish, which she vainly endeavoured to subdue; and a few paces behind the latter, stood another female, whose matron-like appearance retained the traces of a loveliness which in her youth-time must have been of no common order. In the elderly man and this last-mentioned woman, Lorimer instantly recognised James and Mary Doyle—though so many long years had flown since he had last seen them; and in the young female who was clinging to the farmer's arm, it was easy to observe the family resemblance which stamped the daughter of the afflicted couple.

"Yes," continued Lady Lorimer, perceiving that her husband's manner was so bewildered that he could not at the moment give utterance to a word, —"we have our sorrows, good people, as well as you! For you may well suppose that it is not an ordinary affliction which had plunged me into such profound grief when you besought an interview with me ere now,—and which exercises so sad an influence upon Sir Arthur. Alas! twenty-one years have now elapsed since we lost our only son—a lovely, darling boy ——."

"Oh! then, generous-hearted lady," exclaimed

Doyle, turning towards Emily, "you can intercede for *us*—you can understand the terrible woe that wrings our hearts! If Death has deprived you of one so dear ——."

"It was not Death!" said Lady Lorimer, almost suffocated with agonising sobs: "had he died I could have borne it! But to have lost him—to have had him stray from us—perhaps stolen——Oh! my God! the thought drives me mad!"

"Lost your son!—twenty-one years ago!" ejaculated Doyle; and at the same time exclamations of mingled amazement, joy, and terror, burst from the lips of the two females. "What?" continued the man, speaking with strange rapidity and almost wild excitement; — "a boy of about twenty months—dark-eyed and dark-haired—his linen marked A. L.—a mulberry stain on the right arm ——."

"Oh! heaven—what do you mean?" cried Lady Lorimer, clasping her hands together in an agony of suspense.

"Say—what mean you?" demanded the Attorney-

General, springing from the sofa. "Oh! it is impossible — impossible — this hope which you have suddenly excited within me——No—no—do not deceive me! You can have no tidings to give me of my Arthur!"—and the strong, stern, iron-hearted man joined *his* hands also as he gave vent to these broken and impassioned sentences.

"Your Arthur!" shrieked Mrs. Doyle, frantically.

"His son! — Great God! his son!" ejaculated Margaret, falling upon her knees and bursting into a flood of wild weeping.

"Yes—'tis indeed his son," exclaimed the farmer: and, with an expression of countenance so full of horror that no pen could describe—no words depict it, he added in a tone of awful solemnity, "Sir Arthur Lorimer, you have frightful intelligence to hear: for when you so earnestly besought the jury at Exeter to doom Albert Langdon to death, you were pleading against your own child!"

A piercing shriek thrilled from the lips of Lady Lorimer, and she fell senseless upon the floor. At

the same instant a groan, as if of mortal agony, burst
from the Attorney-General; and, staggering back
towards the sofa, he threw himself upon his knees—
buried his head in one of the luxurious cushions—
and gave vent to an anguish which no mortal heart
had ever known before!

CONCLUSION.

It was a long time ere Lady Lorimer was recalled
to life, and ere the other persons assembled in the
library on this memorable Christmas evening could
so far tranquillise their feelings as to enter into ex-
planations of the past. At length it appeared, from
the farmer's brief and touching narrative, that in
the early part of January, 1791 (a few days after
little Arthur's mysterious disappearance) a gipsy
woman, having a child in her arms, sank down in a
dying state at the door of the Doyles' cottage.
Succour was immediately afforded: but her illness
was as overwhelming as it was sudden; and she had
only just time to breathe a few words ere death
closed her lips for ever. Those words, however, conveyed an intimation to the effect that the little boy
who accompanied her, was a strayed child whom she

had found late on the previous Christmas evening at a distance of nearly fifty miles from Exeter. Unable to obtain any clue to its parentage, the Doyles took charge of the poor little stranger; and, finding that his linen was marked with the initials A. L., they bestowed upon him the name of Albert Langdon, after a valued friend whom the farmer had recently lost. The rest may be easily conceived: — Albert and Margaret, the Doyles' daughter and only child, grew up together—loved—and were married; and the thrift of the young woman's parents enabled them to establish the couple in the farm where they were dwelling happily and thriving well at the time when the miscreant Harpinger appeared to bring a withering blight upon their prosperity.

The Attorney-General was stricken down to the very dust by the awful discovery thus made upon this Christmas evening; and in the present incident, as well as in so many past occurrences, his shrinking soul traced the fulfilment of the dying Margaret's warning, which had pursued him like a curse. Humbled—hurled down from the pinnacle of his austere pride—grovelling, as it were, at the feet of those who now beheld his utter self-degradation, the unhappy man confessed the errors of his earlier years; and, while thus unburthening his laden conscience, and revealing all the wondrous circumstances connected with the existence and the appearance of the pixy, he admitted the startling fact that he had appropriated to himself the great bulk of the splendid fortune left by the deceased sister of Mary Doyle. Yes—*this* was the origin of Sir Arthur's wealth; and Lady Lorimer now heard from the lips of her conscience-stricken husband the origin of those riches for which she had ever been at a loss to account.

Relieved by the confession which he had thus made, the Attorney-General's spirits rallied somewhat again; and, enjoining the strictest secrecy concerning all that had transpired, as a necessary preliminary to the course which he intended to adopt in order to save his son's life, he shut himself up in his own chamber for the rest of the night. On the following day it was known throughout the metropolis that Sir Arthur Lorimer had granted a Writ of

Error in respect to the "Exeter rebels;" and the
execution of the extreme sentence of the law was
accordingly suspended. At the same time the Doyles
and Margaret Langdon took their departure homeward; and, on arriving in Devonshire, they immediately obtained an interview with him who was so
dear to them. Then, within the four walls of the
condemned cell, was the secret of the young man's
birth communicated to him, accompanied by the
assurance that, earnestly and zealously as his own
father had implored a jury to send him to the scaffold, so fervently and enthusiastically would that
parent now labour to snatch him from the grasp of
Death!

And this promise was fulfilled. For when the
Writ of Error came to be argued in the course of a
few weeks, the whole country was amazed and the
Government was thunder-stricken by the incompre-
hensible spectacle of the Attorney-General yielding
every point argued by the prisoners' counsel—assist-
ing that counsel with admissions and concessions—
abandoning every strong point on the side of the

prosecution—and at last flinging up his brief, with the indignant declaration that after the new light which had just been thrown on the character of Harpinger, it would be *downright murder* to send Albert Langdon and his co-accused to the scaffold! The result was inevitable—and immediate orders were transmitted to Exeter to set the prisoners at liberty.

The moment this strange judicial proceeding terminated, Sir Arthur Lorimer addressed a brief note to the Prime Minister, resigning the office of Attorney-General; and within an hour after taking this step, he departed for Devonshire, accompanied by his wife.

Another Christmas Day came round: but on this occasion Sir Arthur and Lady Lorimer were not alone. Their son—their dearly beloved and affectionate son—and their daughter-in-law, the beauteous and amiable Margaret, were present at the festive board; and there also were the kind-hearted James and Mary Doyle. To the countenance of Lady Lorimer smiles had come back; and her husband's features expressed a calm contentment and an inward tranquillity which until within the last few months of his chequered life they never had worn. That he was completely happy, we dare not aver: the past was too deeply impressed upon his mind to leave the present and the future altogether unclouded;—but that a profound and sincere contrition had taught him to believe that he had made his peace with heaven, and had therefore smoothed the remainder of his earthly path, we may unhesitatingly affirm. Nor did he tremble as the hour of nine drew near: for he felt an inward assurance that even the shade of Margaret was appeased by his repentance, and that the spirit of her unbaptized child would haunt him no more. And this presaging hope was fulfilled; and the hour passed without the music and without the apparition which had never failed to visit him for so many years before!

In the modest but comfortable dwelling which Sir Arthur and Lady Lorimer had taken at Exeter, they continued to reside until the death of the former,—an event that occurred within a few years after the incidents which have engaged the latter portion of this narrative. Lady Lorimer then took up her abode with her beloved son and her affectionate daughter-in-law; and with them she lived to a good old age, surrounded by the most unwearied attentions, and dying at length in their arms.

James and Mary Doyle have likewise paid the debt of Nature: but Arthur Lorimer (for he adopted his real name on the discovery of his parentage) and his excellent wife are still living; and if they be possessed of great wealth, they use it well and wisely—not as a means of oppression towards the poor who are dependent upon them, but in the working out of many philanthropic views and humane designs. A numerous and fine family of children has sprung up around them; and on a Christmas Day, it would be difficult to find a happier party than that which assembles beneath the hospitable and honoured roof of Arthur and Margaret Lorimer.

But what of the spy—the Government approver —the miscreant who had promoted rebellion, that he might betray the rebels? Plunged into the depths of poverty—loathed and execrated by all who had ever known him, and also by those to whom he was pointed out—spurned, contemned, and spit upon by even the prowling thieves and lowest vagabonds with whom he sought to herd—the accursed Harpinger dragged on a miserable existence for a few short years; until having one night intruded himself into a filty den occupied by the most wretched beggars whose hideous forms haunt the great thoroughfares of the metropolis, he was recognised by the crew and hurled, shrieking in mortal agony, from a second-floor window. Down he fell:—his body was transfixed on the sp railings that fenced the area of the low lodging-house where this horrible tragedy occurred;—and thus perished the Government Approver.

THE END.